# My Life

# By Jesus Christ

# A Story

# My Life
# By Jesus Christ
# A Story

Christopher Miller

QUIET PUBLISHING

LOS ANGELES  Q  TORONTO

My Life By Jesus Christ – A Story
By Christopher Miller

Published by Quiet Publishing

Los Angeles Office 24446 West Valencia Blvd. #7208
Valencia California 91355
Toronto Office 3-304 Stone Road West Suite 415
Guelph Ontario N1H 3H9
www.quietpublishing.com

ISBN            0-9729707-9-7
LCCN            2003091730
SAN             255-2973


Publisher's Cataloging-in-Publication

Miller, Christopher (Christopher D.), 1947-
    My life by Jesus Christ: a story / Christopher Miller
    p. cm.
    Includes bibliographicial references.
    LCCN 2003091730
    ISBN 0-9729707-9-7

1. Jesus Christ--Fiction. 2. Christianity--Origin--Fiction.  I. Title

PS3613.I5325M95 2003    813'.6
                        QBI33-1356

QUIET PUBLISHING

LOS ANGELES  Q  TORONTO

# PROLOGUE

If you have a book with as presumptuous a title as MY LIFE BY JESUS CHRIST, it deserves an explanation, whether it is qualified as 'a story' or not. My own life is as unlike that of Jesus as most. Weakness, failure, regret, all ran ahead of the virtue and hope of my youth.

By a young age I had developed an attitude toward Christianity; intolerance for what I thought was a hypocritical institution incapable of having much value in terms of real, living, Truth.

But I wanted Truth, and I had run out of places to look. For the last twelve years I have examined the Holy Scriptures, the Bible, with some diligence. I was surprised by what I found. There is a Living God. But the entire Christian faith, as it exists in formal groups, seems virtually without a living heart.

There are many kind and wise people in the world who, I think, will gain Deliverance through knowledge of Jesus Christ. Judgment belongs to God. But you do not have to be God to judge the sects of Christendom; we are all entitled to judge our thoughts. They have virtually all fallen prey to exclusivism and self service—the trap of idolatry. It may be true that every group has to form a worldly mask in a practical sense. Unfortunately I have found few able to shatter that mask, when it becomes an identity in Itself, despite the fact this is required by both scripture and wisdom.

So I have written this story, because despite the foolishness of man, God is a wonderful and real thing, and the Sacred Mysteries of Jesus do offer us access to Him. Wherever my story comes into contact with what we know about Jesus, the Scripture has been relied upon. This book considers, and defers to, the entire context of ALL scripture relating to Jesus that is to be found in the Bible. The course of his human travels and the sequence of things he said and did, are faithfully accurate to the Bible.

Whether there is an inspirational factor in the work, I leave you to decide, knowing it is irrelevant until the Final Analysis. But I do know this; there is a lot of Truth in this book.

I thank you,

Christopher Miller

"When these things begin to take place, stand up and lift up your heads, because your redemption is drawing near."

*Luke 21:28*


"And He will send His angels with a loud trumpet call, and they will gather His elect from the four winds, from one end of the heavens to the other"

*Matthew 24:31*

# TABLE OF CONTENTS

Page

# CHAPTER ONE

There was a lot of fanfare around my birth. Of course I really don't remember any of that, but as I grew I learned about it in small, almost shy, increments. My mother felt she had to tell me, but I could see it was more out of a feeling of responsibility than enthusiasm. It was almost as if she didn't believe it herself, like someone who has been told an important secret by a trusted friend, a parent perhaps, someone so close you simply have to believe them, but still, on some level, you are unable to accept that what they have told you is true.

I accepted what she did tell me in the same way. I was interested. I felt a certain excitement and a strong feeling of curiosity, but I sensed that she didn't really want to talk about it and, like any child, I reacted to the underlying instruction I was being given by her, and pretty much forgot about the subject.

As I start this story I want to talk to you about my humanity. I was a person, a human. I don't mean to say I was normal, but life seemed normal to me, and as I was growing up I appeared normal to those around me. A child is special to its mother, and, naturally, I felt that, but I had no sense of being different from other children. There is a lot of misunderstanding and controversy about my nature, but then there is a lot of misunderstanding on this earth about everything. For those of you who believe I was the walking incarnation of God on earth, I ask you to read on a few pages before you give up. You are not completely wrong.

Mankind has an intense desire to understand. The problem is that understanding is a big thing. Understanding itself cannot be truly represented or defined by a word, or a few words, or words at all, but we can talk about understanding, even Truth, in words and that is good. That's what I am going to do as we go along and, hopefully, at the end, we will understand more. After my life as a man a lot of words were written and spoken about me. Words like 'trinity' and 'God' were used, but really these words do not help in understanding me or my life because they represent things so large, so beyond what any man can experience, understand, and then treat as simply a part of his vocabulary, that to use them as simple definitions supposed to apply to me or the meaning of my life is somehow profane.

But to be a man is something we all understand to a greater or lesser degree, and that is what I was, a man. The only difference between me and the rest of the men on this earth is that I did not make the mistake that is measured in millionths of a measure. That is what separates me from the rest of mankind—I was perfect.

To use this first separation—perfection—in comparing me to the many worthy men who have lived would show only a barely discernable division between us. But the fact is that I made no error in my life. All other men do.

There have been, and are, great men, who, if fairly judged by the tools available to mankind, would be equal in the majority of their life to the majority of mine. But make no mistake; from the position of the Spirit of God, one side of the blade falls to life and the other to death, no other subtlety exists.

One is true and alive; the other is gone in the oblivion of dust. And yet the lifetimes themselves could appear, to human evaluation, indistinguishable in virtue. And so it was. I lived as any man, both loved and doubted. I lived the early part of my life hidden in normality, safe from the intensity of man's scrutiny, and equally invisible to his ability to perceive me as something different, something important. It was this side of the equation that I later found most difficult. I enjoyed the anonymity of being human, but trying to show the truth of the other possibility, the possibility that I was different, perhaps imperceptibly, but essentially, proved to be an illumination of how well the truth is guarded from the approach of man's understanding.

As a child my first memories were of Egypt. Big, colorful, and from my position on my mother's back, noisy, dusty, and wonderful.

It was custom among my people to shelter the young, especially the first born boy, so, be it a small room hidden from crowded streets, or fur rugs and woven wool placed off beside the fire, I grew up in a protected realm, the world of my mother. A world of serenity and beauty and brilliant mornings; in the darkness of the early night quiet flames brought contented drowsiness. They were days full of women and food, color and laughing eyes, all busy about some duty that led from kiss to kiss and hug to hug.

I was very young when my family decided to move back to Judea; three; perhaps a little younger when they first started packing. To me the journey was pretty much a blur, camels and bags, everyone moving in confused crowded ways, until the chaos settled to a slowly turning wheel of people, sky and sand, finally spilling out into the desert and the vast lonely confines of travel.

We never arrived at our intended destination, Judea. I remember late night talks between my mother and father, talks that assumed I was asleep, talks that rose and sank in intensity, with words and hidden lamps that I knew were unusual to the normal flow of night. I suppose that during one of those talks it was decided to change direction, and we went to Nazareth, not Bethlehem. I later learned that Archelaus, the new king of Judea, was as virulently concerned about the religious rumors of a Jewish Messiah, as was his father, Herod, making Judea dangerous for us.

Nazareth was a small, unnoticed city, perched in the hills and valleys of Galilee. It was a beautiful place, perfect in the ways that only the memories of childhood can maintain. Since it was the village where my parents had lived before I was born, we settled into a home and a world that were familiar and easily accepted. My mother and father were less concerned with the rough physical environment than with the establishment of their hearth, a hearth protected and nurtured by the living light of the world's True Creator.

Nazareth looked over a gently curved valley, extending into the haze of the distance, with much of the town sprawling into the shallow bowl of the valley and surrounded by a symmetry of hills that made the area so identifiable. It was a city or a village depending on who you were, small in comparison to the fortified cities of Japhia or Sepphoris which were both near by, but close to the trade routes, busy, and always up to date on the latest news of activities, both political and religious.

We took up residence in a small house near the outskirts of the town, close enough for my father to buy his materials and attract some notice for his trade, but away from the narrow jostled streets of the market. By the time I was six I would be taken by my father to his workshop for a morning or an afternoon, sitting quietly and watching, even occasionally being asked to hand him a tool or a piece of wood. I loved the shop. I loved the smell of the different woods stored carefully above our heads in measured stacks to dry and await the moment they would be pulled out and fashioned by Joseph's skilled hands. I loved the golden light that filled the room as the warm sun found its way from one window to the other, touching the benches and the curious tools, clamps with threaded batons that tightened to perfect grip, and smooth handled adzes made lustrous with use and the oils from my father's hands. The ochre walls held the light, still friendly long after the direct sunlight had left the room.

As I grew older my cautious help became more and more frequent, until I received duties rather than requests, and the time spent with my father became routine instead of occasional. I think this was the happiest time of my life, although by ten my mind and eyes were often fastened on the hills and trees outside the window, and I was distracted by a quiet fiery joy that waxed and waned between my heart and head.

The joy I felt came from spirit. The ability I had to feel that joy without question or insecurity came from the faith of my people and from my parent's comfortable dedication to that faith. By the time I was beginning to remember things, our religious life had settled down to routines that had been practiced by Jews since the time of Moses. And that meant that our life was based on the scriptures, and the resulting knowledge of God. To the upright and faithful Jew, which my parents and their parents had always been, God and the Law were as real a part of their daily life as the things of the earth. Food, air, love, anger, light, God, worship, study, worry, fatigue, sleep, were all simply part of their life. If asked, a Jew would of course place God above all other things, but in fact God was a fibre of the rope that made up existence and that was that.

I loved this devotion, and accepted it and expected it just as I did our meals, and it was no coincidence that our meals were times when God and faith were inevitably as present as the food and utensils themselves. Each morning my father would read from the scripture, and we would listen. Sometimes my mother would ask a question, or point out that my father could apply such wisdom to such and such a task, a little mischievous twinkle in her eye as she said it, my father smiling to himself and shaking his head, bringing us back to the more serious nature of the text. When the reading and prayer were done we carried on to the meal without pause, the contentment in our hearts a little stronger. It was scripture, prayer, and food that brought us back to the center, after a morning or afternoon of worldly frustrations that would tire and confuse more often than not. Whether I was with my father in the shop or walking with him to the market, if I was sitting with my mother at noon or resting on her lap after the evening meal, God was never far away. Some little detail of life would always bring up a comparison to a proverb or a law; a lesson on patience, a gratitude for a beauty brought to notice, a warning as to how the hurry caused the pain, or the lack of attention caused a distress or sadness, our recognition of this little mistake a reason to be thankful to our creator. On the Sabbath, though, we truly focused on religion. When I was old enough, and that wasn't very old, I had to struggle to read the scriptures themselves, and remember the books and their order, and what the essential elements of each book or section were. I had to memorize certain scriptures according to a method and order passed down to my father as the recommended course of study, the one given to his father and his father's father. When my brothers and sisters came along I watched as both my mother and father lovingly and with a kind of proud but serene elation repeated the lessons to each in turn. I also couldn't help but notice, especially from my mother, how they sometimes stared at me as I repeated some verse or other, or smiled at some comment I made, and how my mother often talked to me about the things she felt most closely, be they troubles or satisfactions, or questions about the deeper aspects of life. Some of this I knew was because I was the firstborn, but I also knew that some of it came from the things we rarely discussed, that God had told my mother that I was important to Him, that I was in fact His son, and destined to rule over all of Israel. My mother had only told me these things once, with perhaps a few more details and references, like little asterisks, just to make sure she had done her duty to the truth. And why not with reticence, for what mother would be foolish enough to seriously believe her child was the Son of God, the King destined to rule over the earth for eternity? It made a mockery of reason, not to mention humility. We simply did not mention these things, but we both knew they had been said. When I noticed my mother staring into the far distance I knew that in the hidden heart of mind and soul she was remembering those times not so long ago when, as she had told me, an angel had spoken to her about my birth and life. Perhaps the fact that most held her reverie was the fact she was a virgin on the day of my birth; my very existence indisputable evidence of mystery.

To talk about my life begins with explaining my birth. To explain my birth is to talk about God, about our reality, and about why my birth was so important to the earth.

# CHAPTER TWO

One way to describe God is through images. God Itself is not really definable. Ezekiel gives us a description of God that is useful, but it does not attempt to place God in perspective to our immediate reality. The powerful images of his scripture portray God in His attribute as a manifestation with a persona in time and space, as if God was at one place at one time. Most humans long for a time when such a view of God can be realized, but this will not occur in our world. What is worthwhile for human beings is to have an understanding of God that positions Him in relationship to the categories of life we are familiar with, the physical, emotional, and cognitive universe around us, and most importantly this understanding must be in the context of the full duration of our lives.

In the search for an image that may help with this kind of understanding it is natural to look to the world and universe we see and to the descriptions of this universe supplied by our thinkers. The most accepted of such descriptions is accurate enough to begin with.

Our universe began with a massive explosion of energy. As the energy moved outward from the center it began to assemble itself as fundamental matter. Great clouds of this matter condensed to form areas that displayed force as gravity. As the strength of gravity increased stars were born. Stars came together as galaxies. Stars gave off their own force as light, the energy that brought and sustains life. Many are convinced that over a complete age of time the galaxies of our universe ultimately lose their momentum, pause, virtually lifeless and expended, to begin the inevitable journey back to the center that originally disgorged them. As the galaxies are pulled back to their source they pick up speed. The center gains density as galaxy upon galaxy approach it. Gravity increases as the stars converge. Soon there is no separation between stars; ultimately there is no space between atoms. There is only mass and energy. The gravity is so strong that even light may not be emitted; the energy is so powerful that no gravity may contain it. The struggle between infinite opposites is resolved in a catastrophic eruption that hurls the raw elements of energy into the emptiness of space. The universe is born again and so it goes.

Some of the deeper thinkers of our world have added an important elaboration to this theory. Meditation that combined pure thought with the awareness of living elements of consciousness brought about conclusions that could not be denied. Early mystics realized that there was a certain unity between points; points that appeared to be separated by distance. A movement of energy felt within a person sitting in quiet meditation might cause the thinker to open his eyes, and in so doing notice an undeniable connection between the sensations of invisible movement he was experiencing with the sudden unanimous puff of motion as a flock of small birds took to the air. Over time similar observations and awareness brought about conclusions that seemed likely to apply to the universe in general. One such supposition was that if the universe expands and contracts, perhaps there is a unity over time that includes and transcends the apparent separation between the stages of such an evolution.

Similar thinking led to a more sophisticated understanding of reality than the linear concepts man uses to fashion his collective approach to life. What is sometimes called non-dualistic thought holds that the center of the universe in its fully contracted position, the momentary equilibrium between two great opposite forces that precedes the birth of the universe is, in fact, always in existence. The center is always infinitely complete, remaining intact beyond time but giving the appearance of movement and change through time and space.

The apex of modern thought seems to agree, some would say paradoxically, with these ancient contemplations. Mathematics hints at the validity of such concepts. It is generally accepted that as mass approaches the speed of light, time, as experienced by that object, is shortened. The proverbial space traveler, moving at close to the speed of light, travels to a distant spot and returns a few years later to find the world a thousand years older. As he approached the speed of light time slowed down for him. Time and matter as we know it virtually cease at the speed of light. An imaginary traveler essentially becomes light when he reaches the speed of light. He exists both at the source and at the very end of the ever outwardly moving ray at the same instant. His position is determined by consciousness. Since there is no time at light speed, it is not important how long it takes to move from the source of the beam of light to the midpoint, or anywhere along the ray. All points along, or within the ray exist at once. We simply are at one spot or another according to awareness. So with the center of all things; it is always there, in all its stages. All reality exists in this center, this first and final stage, which doesn't move, or change. It is awareness within this center that determines where we are along the illusion of time and space.

Consonant with the true condition of the world, neither the mystical nor the empirical have succeeded in one of their foremost purposes, proving that the universe is this unified singularity.

I make no such attempt here. Actual proof, we learn, exists only as Truth makes its entrance into reality.

To talk about God is no simple thing. To read about God requires perseverance.

"God is a Spirit."[1] God is first Itself. God Itself recognizes Itself partially as Spirit so that it can be present as separate. The Spirit of God is invisible in terms of what we call vision. We know that vision is dependant on light, and light is composed of energy in a form that does not even comprise the full spectrum of physically detectable energy. The Spirit can manifest an image that we can see as humans, but what we see is not The Spirit. The Spirit exists in and beyond all things.

What we know as our universe began when God willed it. According to His will, Spirit extended and divided itself to make its first appearance in physical form as the hydrogen atom. Within this atom existed the beginning, evolution, and completion of all things material, although it contained no limitation. Within the poles of duality that begin with this atom is found the cause of all that follows as matter. It contains the genome, you might say, of our universe. It contains all of the physical laws, as evidenced by the precise arrangement, characteristics, and behaviour of all elements as they appear on the periodic table. Not only is this atom well represented by the number one, it has more substantial symbols. It is the seed of the tree that we know as life. It is the embryo, the infant is the universe, and the parent that nurtures that infant to adulthood is the spirit.

The spiritual force, separated, redesigned, and bound within this atom, emerged in abundance. In the early movements of its majestic dance it partially reunited, giving off energy and light, and forming more complex matter. When spirit began this action it did not do so outside of itself. Its apparent transformation at the will of God used only a fraction of its totality. What we perceive as empty space is actually spirit itself, the womb of physical creation.

Strictly speaking our universe has no center. From a physical standpoint it has many centers, many points where the massive energies of creation appear in such concentration that each one is capable of fathering a cycle of galactic expansion and contraction as described in our model. It is understandable that from the perspective of man we expect a center, and there is one. There is only one center, and of course that is what we call God. It is true when we say that God is the one true center. It is more accurate to say that God is both within and without. A portion of God takes form as the atoms that comprise matter and the energy matter exudes. It is God as spirit that permeates both the seen and the unseen to guide the creation of the final perfect shapes our universe adopts. And it is God that exists beyond the illusion of both.

Many refer to our life as illusion. Once again, words can often take away more than they give. Life is real. Our pain is real. But it is not incorrect to say that life, especially on the earth, is an illusion. Man's universe, from our perspective, does exist in the form of time and space, in the form of stars and galaxies and the centers of force that create them. Time and space display themselves as fullness and emptiness, but even in the moment of our observation of them they are unified beyond time and space, through the nature of what they are, spiritual force. What we perceive as light, and then as life, and then as time, do exist. They exist just as a circle of luminosity exists when a strong beam of light is cast against a dark surface. The source of that existence, none the less, is the flashlight. If the consciousness of the True Center does not include our universe, we simply cease, as the circle of light disappears when the flashlight is turned off. The disappearance is as absolute as the end of a flicker. But it is Its will that we be, and we shall.

I would like to use this context to explain why miracles are so simple for God. As an example we can use the miracles preformed by Moses as the Nation of Israel left the bondage of Egypt. If a miracle is required to further God's intent for the earth, spirit simply awakens itself within an atom in the body of the instrument being used to bring the required effect about. That atom then releases sufficient energy to influence other atoms spread about the physical area where the miracle is to be preformed and they exert the appropriate energies to initiate the action. Spirit in its pervasive form as the Mover then relaxes the laws of physics that normally prevail. Energies are then exchanged between whatever atoms are necessary and the miracle occurs, say, the Red Sea parts. When the time sequence is complete the natural laws are reimposed on the field involved. Miracles initiated by God are not frequent, as we see from the record of scripture. Miracles can be initiated by men, I was able to use them freely, but they were prompted by pure motives. In duality all actions, miracles included, have effects. Most attempts by human beings to call upon the power of spirit do not include an accurate perspective, and spirit does not respond. Even miracles condoned by God but carried out by an imperfect mind have their cost. It is good to realize that any increase in positive energy leaves a corresponding area where negative energy can proportionately increase. A good example of this can be seen in the very different energies that exerted themselves simultaneously, around Moses while he was on the mountain top, on the one hand, and around the Hebrew camp while he was gone, on the other.

In this explanation I have used the word duality. The heart of the matter is here. God exists within and without in universal duality. God more importantly exists in the vast universes of pure spirit, beyond duality, where I was first born. To Man, at the present moment, universal duality is not attainable. The entire physical universe exists in a perfect balance, originating in the atom and guided by spirit. The only exception to this is Earth, temporarily separated from the universe by the fact that it is controlled by flawed spirit. Visible light, Spirit, and Truth are links for us, to both the universe and God, but we are impotent to Creation until I bring liberation.

Before God manifested himself as this heart of either the physical or spiritual universe He was Himself alone. At some point He created something that was other than Himself. What he created was called the Word, His Son. And when He did this He made Me. I was the creature of spirit that was to have awareness of all the stages of universe and yet remain separate from them all. I was the first creation. I was the first point of awareness actually separate from God. Although all things are made up of forces and particles created from the energies of God, it was the desire of God that some things actually be independent; in union with, but distinct from, God Itself. In a way, man clumsily imitates this intention when he looks toward creating artificial intelligence. I was the first of these forms and, as I said, in the beginning I was simply a point of awareness. But unlike man's attempts at creation I was complete at the moment of my inception, not finished by a long shot, but complete in absolute perfection to grow and expand in all aspects to the infinite realization and expression of my nature. Thereafter I was the consciousness used to assist with the formation of all things extra to God.

As the first creation I was active in everything that followed. I moved back and forth along the streams of the spiritual worlds, both being and creating. Now let's understand one thing, truth may be simple in its heart, but along the way to understanding it can be very complicated, to say the least. Many men have pointed out that Reality is the thing itself and that no set of words however perfect can define or explain Reality. And it is pretty obvious that words simply add themselves to reality as they are spoken or written and do little more. Fewer men have pointed out that two seemingly contradictory things can both be true. They can be true at different times, under different circumstances, or both at the same time. That is why I can say that words are simply words and are only a tiny aspect of reality and also say that some words are so powerful that they shape and define Reality, even become Reality itself, and be correct in both statements. Keeping this liberating qualification in mind, I bring you to a time that was neither young in terms of my existence nor old enough to deny its newness as a moment. It was a time when the universe of which I was a part had created a variation of itself that was true to its nature but laden with complexity. This complexity of matter limited the creation to a set of specific points in both time and space, but mechanisms were in place that would allow for the advancement of that creation into a more spiritual, and thus infinite, form. Almost immediately upon its release from the transitory grasp of creation (what we call evolution) to the reality of freedom of being (what we call the Garden of Eden) this 'world' encountered a hitherto unmanifested aspect. Without being detected by the universe or highlighted by spirit, a moment arose when one of the spiritual beings used in the creation of this world had a dialogue with a new born free inhabitant of this world that shocked the forces interlocked with that moment throughout the universe. The dialogue went like this:

Do you have choice?

*Yes.*

Are there any limitations to your choice?

*There is one limitation.*

What is that?

*I may not perform one action.*

Why?

*If I do I will cease to exist.*

Who will enforce this rule?

*The One who created us.*

What if by performing this act you become one with the one that created you?

*I suppose I would not die, since that one, the Creator, will not die.*

I tell you as a creature of the True Reality, if you perform this action you will become like the creator. Is this, then, a true limitation?

*It does not seem so.*

Here the spirit creature implies that God has lied, that breaking the rule will not mean death, but the opposite, a kind of equality with God. This implies, further, that the 'rule' was made for God's benefit, keeping the gift of equality away from the human creation, and was, as such, a selfish action.

If it is not True can it be to your benefit?

*It would not appear so.*

Will you then do this act and thus go beyond limitation?

*I may.*

And in fact she did.

And thus a twofold question was raised.

Does the Creator have a valid moral right to impose a rule upon his creation?

If He does impose a rule, is it for the benefit of the creator or the creation that this rule is made?

Until both questions are answered, neither answer would be complete.

The response of this 'new' creation gave the questions themselves

Reality that transcended simple 'knowledge', and had to be answered in same coin they were asked, through the actuality of action. The Truth was that the Creator had not lied in His warning as to the consequences of eating of the fruit of the tree of the knowledge of good and bad, and thus the human creations, the individuals that took the action requiring death, did die. In the manner common to universal law, the death was not brought about by any overt action meant to enforce the original rule, but occurred through the silent force of the True Reality which is active in all ways on all levels. The action of doing what was forbidden by the Creator was an error, and error is not possible in a perfect universe, and so, to remain perfect this error had to cease to exist in the universe. Error cannot grow out of itself into perfection, since the seed of error does not contain perfection. The seed of error creates further error that grows until it finds itself in conflict with what is True. Since it is not True it ultimately ceases to be and the universe remains in errorless perfection. And so man and woman died.

But the seeds of error continued in the form of their children and in the now imperfect environment distorted by error, called the earth or the world. These children were doomed by the imperfection they were, although they had done nothing in particular, at birth, to place themselves as subject to destruction. But they would die nonetheless.

What was God to do?

God did what was perfect.

First it was established that He would allow the spirit creature that took part in the questioning of the creatures of creation, along with the humans themselves that took action as a result of the questioning, to have the full benefit of the creation to themselves, without only God's will and guidance, in order to answer the second question without the undue influence of God. The second question raised by the dialogue of deception was: Was the original rule for the benefit of God or creation?

This question is not yet fully answered and until it is, the first question remains.

Only when this world has come to a point where it is either perfect by its own evolution, or, doomed by this same unfolding, and only when either condition is evident to all definitions of intelligence in the universe, will this question be answered. Only then will the truthfulness, purity of, and necessity for, God's rule denying premature knowledge of duality to the human being be vindicated.

The answer to this question will also answer the first of the two questions raised by the dialogue of the spirit creature with the first man and woman, 'Does the creator have a right to make a rule for its creation?'

If the creation returns to a viable, and thus perfect, place in the universe, then the rule is superfluous, and the answer to the first question, 'Does God have the right to make a rule for his conscious creations,' would be defendable as, no. The creation will have proved to be capable of sustaining itself in a good way without subjection to the creator.

If the creation spirals further and further down into pain and despair and ultimately destruction, then the rule was justified, even necessary, and makes the answer to the question, unequivocally, Yes. Although this point of no return was nearly reached at the time of the flood, there remained redeeming qualities in mankind, in Noah, that moved mankind's destiny forward to a more complete scrutiny, thereafter without the intimate interference of angels, whether faithful to either God or Satan.

The history that follows the flood is our grappling with these two basic questions, the answers to which form the only true goal of reason, a fact that eludes all but a handful of Christians and Truth Seekers. Suffering on this earth is not the result of some hidden purpose of God, but purely and simply the result of the fact that this world is in the hands of men and spirit creatures, without the active direction of the living spirit of God, which is the director and sustainer of universal harmony. Suffering and death are neither part of God's plan nor workings of His will. They are simply the result of error-filled actions that are inevitable in the situation the earth finds itself in, while, and until, the questions asked by that original dialogue are answered once and for all time.

When this question, of whether God's rule is a benefit to the creation, is answered, as it will be soon, the chaos and pain and cruelty and ignorance that abound on this planet will never again be tolerated by the active presence of God, for any reason, at any time, at any place. We may be certain that the answer to the question is affirmative. This uncertain world will not survive without reconciliation with the God of which it is a part. I talk about this throughout the book, as I do about the things I think are important to understand, and different context will help, I hope, to make complex things simple.

So why was I born to man?

Well, the answer is that while the two fundamental questions of universal justice I have spoken about are being answered by the only means possible—cause and effect proven through time and space—another question had arisen concerning mankind.

The children of the original man and woman were now imperfect in an imperfect world, and no longer under the spiritual guidance of the will of God. They were going to make errors and the errors were going to mean death. But could they choose not to make an error, could they choose to obey the singular regulation imposed on their parents by the Creator and thus not die? No. They were now irreversibly trapped in a world not envisioned by the original intentions of creation, a world as real and inescapable as it was imperfect and separated from universal wisdom.

This situation violated the absolute perfection of universal truth, and consequently God added a caveat to his 'hands off' approach to the future of the world. He would offer advice and guidance to one man on the earth at all times. Through this guidance of one man, He would offer deliverance to all men who lived on the face of this imperfect world, although this was secret in the beginning.

The 'one man' exception was tacitly agreed to by the spirit creature that was eager to inherit dominion over the earth, and so our history began.

But how was this relationship with only one man going to offer salvation to a mankind now moving further and further away from an accurate memory or knowledge of God? Of course, as most of you know in a very facile way, this is where I came in.

From my position as a co-creator, I had watched in sorrow as the things I discussed above transpired. I watched the couple leave the finished garden and I spoke in silent thought to the angel placed to guard the tree, all the heavens heavy with the grief and pain of anguish yet unborn but certain. The voice of my Father began to take the shape of things to come, and as it is in the worlds of truth, the future, past, and present danced together in a mild ecstasy, and I both saw, and prepared to do, what was being brought from creative force to embryonic reality. All that I had ever been, all that I had ever known, every connection to the timeless universe I loved and lived within, all were fading. I lost my life as spirit and fell, spinning, drowning, spinning into the darkness of the womb, a new and unformed life, a tabula rasa of flesh and spirit, an infant, a man. But I was no normal child of this imperfect earth; I was a man with all the attributes of the first man. I was perfect, as were the first human couple the universe had created. Like them I was flawless, faultless, and capable of choosing once again between the options of obedience and disobedience. I could answer the question of whether to obey God or not, for myself, whereas all other men born of women suffered with the reality that their existence itself was the result of the answer given by their ancestors. They were incapable of choosing from the position of perfection, as I was able to do, and thus doomed to answering in the negative by the proof of their imperfect actions. And my answer never needed to be spoken, because the question itself has no meaning other than the choice of negativity itself, which I was not inclined to make.

So there it is, often alluded to but little understood. I was not God. But I was not imperfect, as were all men of human birth before and after me. I was perfect, as was Adam.

Now since the essence of my being was placed within the womb, complete and perfect, by the spirit of God, I was perfect when I emerged from the womb into the very imperfect world. To be perfect means a lot of things we are not here to define, but one of its aspects is that its inertia is to not make a mistake. Since the world I was born into had been given Law, by God, I was under this law in the same manner as any other Jew. It was through the law that all Jews had evidence of their condemnation, for no imperfect man could perfectly obey the law. To obey the law perfectly it was appropriate for me to know the law completely, and indeed I was born to a life that would allow me this knowledge.

As I pointed out before, God was intrinsic to the life of a Jew. We were Israel. Israel was a Nation God called His own. It might seem a bit unfair for God to limit himself to direct contact with one man or women at a time and then extrapolate that to include a nation of millions, but His relationship was subtly different with Israel. The single man God chose along the line of our history, as recorded in the Bible, was always a man perceived by God as being capable of understanding the true nature of existence. This man was charged with keeping Truth alive in the conscious moment, even if that was done imperfectly. The important thing was that God had the right to a direct relationship with one man at a time. This relationship varied in its nature as God saw fit, but it always included an accurate knowledge of Who God was, and a direct connection with God that ensured the man would be able to preserve his faith to the end of his life. When God chose the one man Abram, he established a relationship with that man that was part of the mystery of the salvation of the World. God renamed Abram, Abraham, and he became a more important figure than most of the lineage as did Moses, Elijah, and David. God asked Abraham to sacrifice his son. This misunderstood request, often thought of as barbaric, was actually one of the most important moments in our history. It would allow God to proceed with our deliverance without deviating from His own perfect justice. Fortunately the action of Abraham, in his compliance, made God's design to send me to the earth lawful. Abraham was willing to offer his son's life to God, and thus it was justified for God to offer his own Son's life to man. And this He did. I want you to understand this: I didn't bring my celestial identity to the earth all rolled up in the form of flesh. I died as the singularity God had created billions of years before. I retained the original point of awareness that is uniquely me, but all memory and experiential growth were gone. Without this death my life on earth would have meant little, as it would have been defined as merely the interference of a powerful spiritual creature with the affairs of the world, allowing the forces in opposition to God to do the same, with a resulting negation of benefit.

So Abraham became a pivot in the destiny of this world. It was in the context of God's relationship with Abraham that He promised to look after Abraham's progeny in a personal way, to see that they prospered. The children of a man are part of that man in

God's eyes, because the man exists genetically in the child, so the relationship with the Nation of Israel was intimate, although not equal to the bond God allowed Himself with the select individuals, who represent the seed of Eve. This promise concerning the seed of Abraham was made more specific when God solidified and clarified His covenant with Abraham as pertaining to the offspring of Jacob, Abraham's grandson who was later renamed Israel. And so, from then on, all the descendents of Israel were the People of God, as the sons of Abraham, not simply for a few generations, but, hopefully, in perpetuity. Thus God's involvement in the affairs of this world grew from the private relationship with one select person to include the parental tutelage of a nation, the seed of one man, Israel. It was, because of its limited nature, never a very satisfactory relationship, and God always maintained the fire of truth itself within one individual, as recorded, down throughout the years until it lead to, and ended with, me. But God's connection with Israel enabled me to be educated in and raised under the Law of God, and the truth is, that is all that mattered. That is part of the divine mystery of the Scripture, revealed only by my death, and then divulged as the Good News.

I have talked about God, about reality, about Israel, about my birth and why it was important to both the earth and the universe, because some understanding of these things is necessary for my life to be of any real interest.

I was born a Child of Israel. This meant I was involved with God. Beyond the daily involvement with God that I shared with my parents, I was, as were all Hebrew children, carefully nourished and educated in the truth by the community as a whole. We had the synagogue, we had the Sabbath, we had the festivals, and we had school.

The Sabbath was a thing unique to our people, but then so was our God. To most tribes and nations of the world God was something that came along separately, a product of their politics and nationalism. They created their God with chisel and temple. The God they imagined, then created, became the God that existed for them. This may seem a bit simplistic, but it is a point that reappears regardless of how deep you dig. To us God was a thing outside our nation. The nations created their Gods at whim, with the exception of the children of Ishmael, who share the same God as the Jews, though neither seem to truly understand that. He existed before and separate from us, in fact, He had chosen us, not we Him, and to keep Him in our lives we had to live according to the Law He had given us. The Sabbath exemplified this. This day was devoted entirely to worship, to remembering the creator of heaven and earth. It was a day when any kind of work or labor was absolutely forbidden, every moment was to be devoted to worship and thought, to reading and study, to feasting and enjoyment. It was a cheerful day, it had decorum, yes, but it was a time of celebration and love.

The synagogue was a slight departure from the law, in the sense that strictly speaking we were all supposed to worship at the temple in Jerusalem. The realities of the time made this virtually impossible and within the newly fashioned traditions of the local scribes and Pharisees came the institution of the synagogue. Despite a lack of formal acknowledgement from the aristocrats of the temple in Jerusalem, every Jewish town or city had a synagogue. It was here the Pharisees and the learned men of each community gathered to worship and learn. It was here the men and women sat on the floor, separately, to recite the shema, to pray, to read from the law and to read from the prophets, and to hold discourse on what had been read. Although the synagogues had rulers, any worthy person could, and did, read and discuss the holy writings. It was here, on the morning after the families had answered the summons of the trumpet announcing the Sabbath, and returned to their homes to feast, sing, and pray, enjoying their finest clothes and finest wine and purest feelings, that the community met to worship and celebrate the day devoted to the living God.

It was at the synagogue that I attended school. I didn't like having to leave my mother's side, and I missed the long mornings with my father in the workshop, where I was becoming, at least I thought, more and more useful. But there were lots of other children at school, and as I realized that a full understanding of the sacred writings was a larger task than I had imagined, and as I began to understand the methodical approach we would take to guarantee a thorough study, I started to get excited about the prospect of truly learning about God. Jews had no need for secular study. We had everything we thought was important to life within the context of our religion. We had language, we had poetry and geography, and we had the transcendent joy of reaching understandings about ourselves and the world that reached into the very center of life. My young contemporaries and I began to feel the power of our God reaching into our hearts and minds, and soon everything we saw with our eyes was filtered through the mysterious light of a power more tangible and real to us than the signs of material power we were beginning to notice in the temporal world around us. At least I saw it that way, and I think so did the other boys in one way or another, but where the interest grew to boredom for some of my friends, my passion only increased with knowledge, and by the time I was twelve I felt more than ready to accept the mantle of adulthood, and to embrace the full responsibility for my actions as judged by the God of Israel.

I had learned a lot in school. I had grown from a child to a young adult, and my understanding of the world reflected this change. It is not too well known that the intellectual peak of a man is reached in the year or two before the changes brought about by adolescence begin to rob him, hormonally, of the full use of his brain. Of course in terms of knowledge and wisdom, like most men, I grew wiser and more knowledgeable as I grew older, but in terms of sheer energy and acuity my mind was never better than in the years during which I was taken to the temple in Jerusalem to formally acknowledge my entrance into adulthood. I knew from my own studies that I was soon to be responsible for my personal observance of the Law of God, and I took this very seriously.

I had learned so much! I was so full of enthusiasm and excitement. I had learned from the scriptures about how the universe had an intelligent, no, an all-intelligent creator, a real person, not a physical person of course, but a real person nonetheless, an aware, caring individual, a loving and powerful master of existence, as wise as all wisdom, and as kind and understanding as you would wish to be with yourself. I had learned how mankind had been cheated out of a joyful destiny, how the perfection of the world had been spoiled, and how the unity and freedom that should have blown through the earthly kingdom, through blossom and dew, through morning and treetop, through softness and beauty, through the simple dignity and beauty of the animals, had been lost. I knew that spirit-filled harmony should have transmuted the earnest thoughts of men into physical reality, the gift of worldly dominion given to man by a loving God. This gift of creativity should have allowed man to complete the patterns of life as it had been intended, as it had been woven throughout the eons of endless time. All this had been lost.

I had learned and thought about this, and then I had learned about it on a deeper level, even as a child. I had seen and felt the little moments where, even for the fortunate, the true gravity of our human plight breaks through into that moment of physical, emotional, and intellectual awareness we call realization, or whatever word we should use to describe moments of deep insight. I had felt the shock and then the icy grip of nausea that held my stomach for an instant as fear flashed through my body, leaving me cold and empty, with only my thoughts to pull me back to the quiet contentment of normality. Even in Nazareth, this underlying discomfort was there, not obvious, but there. I had seen the flash of violence as a Roman soldier struck a lethal blow to a man who suddenly seemed pathetic and helpless, who had just a moment before stood proud and critical, although perhaps a little too confident in his feeling of moral correctness. I had seen the foulness of impending death as a ravished body was whisked away to some barren sanctuary outside the city walls. I had seen the eyes of women, men, and children so filled with despair and hopelessness that even death could seem a welcome friend. I had seen the filth of poverty and neglect; even by the age of eight or nine I had seen enough to know that something was very wrong.

But the brightness of my youth covered the lasting effects of these things, for I had also read the promises of scripture and prophet, and I knew that God would fix the problems. In fact I was more excited than worried about the prospects of what was to come, as much from the simple optimism of the young as from my own nature, and I pushed into my life, anxious to observe and be a part of the great events that the majority of my community talked about and yearned for. And this was deliverance, the deliverance of my people. It was deliverance from Rome and deliverance from the shackles of a dark world, deliverance, in fact, for the entire world, brought about by the hand of God. It manifested as a feeling and a force that ran through virtually all of us in Galilee, anticipation.

So perhaps you can understand how happy I was when my parents told me that they would be taking me to Jerusalem for the Passover. I knew the trip wasn't entirely for me—every family planned and saved to make the trip as often as they could—but I also knew it was no accident that my first trip to Jerusalem coincided with my coming of age.

After the Passover at Jerusalem I would be a man. Not a mature man of course, but I would be responsible to God for my own self, no longer attached to my parents in matters of conscience or, yes, sin. I was proud about this, and I wanted to put my feelings of confidence and devotion to God to the test. There were things that I had noticed that had bothered me, some serious, like the common and often attractive rhetoric of the young men, though older than me by far, who talked about taking up the sword to free our people from the iron grip of Rome. Their arguments were convincing, and it seemed the scriptures to some extent backed them up, for every Jew knew that bondage was not our natural destiny, and I noticed that even the older men smiled and nodded their heads approvingly when a passing orator would stir the crowds to passionate longing for action and the freedom it could bring. But my parents did not share such views, and I was uncomfortable with them myself, but now, as a man I could talk and think and argue with the agitators and the pacifists alike. I would decide; and the thought of finding out what was truly correct for me, and my people, thrilled me, as much for the journey of learning as for the conclusions it would bring. Some of the things that puzzled me seemed less important on the surface than the issues of nationalism, but, as it turned out, were more symptomatic of the web of error that holds man so desperately captive. The pride of the congregation leaders, who seemed to miss the point sometimes, but still managed to suffocate the enthusiasm of budding thought, confused me. They were so quick to dismiss the value of men and women less recognized by public position, rejecting sincere ideas with disdain, citing platitudes often more fashionable than correct. I looked forward to my task as an adult to really learn the truth about these things, and now that time was coming, although I certainly didn't know then, like all the young, just how long it would be before I truly answered most of these questions.

# CHAPTER THREE

The party gathering for the journey was large. I could hardly contain my joy, everyone looked so beautiful. The sky and sand were more vivid and sparkling that ever, the power and feel of the coming spring seeming to shine out of the younger of us as if we simply couldn't hold it in. Even the older men, though busy with the camels and the stores, laden with the wonderful equipment of the full-grown man, leather and silver, metal and jangling loops and polished sword and heavy water bags, couldn't contain their good humor, flashing smiles and bright commands to the boys who scurried around, and whispering silent, mysterious messages to the women who flowed through the growing camp, effortlessly weaving the chaos into a caravan of color and purpose. It was good, and many friendly eyes met mine, sharing in an instant a wave of common understanding and shared happiness.

We took the directly southern route to Jerusalem, through Samaria. I didn't know exactly why. It was more common to circle east across the Jordan; the Samaritans were not known for their friendliness to Jews, but apparently there was trouble on the more traveled path, and Roman soldiers—especially if they may have thought of us as connected in any way to remnants of recent uprisings—were more to be feared than any other danger, and in any case the southern route was shorter. It was obvious to me that nothing was going to dampen the optimism of our group. I knew the older men had no real concern about our safety, so with an almost uncontainable enthusiasm we set out for Jerusalem, the City of God, the site of the temple, the home of God on earth.

I was in such high spirits that time seemed to fly. A lot of the children were my age, about seven of us scattered throughout the camp, but Rachael, the daughter of a friend of my mother's, was the only one really close to me. Her appearance always seemed to bring a smile to my face. Her long soft wool tunic, with thin vertical stripes of bright orange, dull and dusty golds and dark blues, with wider stripes of muted maroon edged with black and grey and umber so familiar to my people, at least in Nazareth, stirred deep and happy feelings. She was thin and lithe, her long black hair set off by even blacker eyes that flashed a visible light, rising and falling in intensity with her mood and enthusiasm. The only occasions when time seemed to slow down were when Rachael was close. Our eyes would meet on their random sweeps around the moving line of people, and often she would sit beside me, our legs dangling off the back of a cart, or huddled down in the shade of the driver's seat to avoid the high sun. We didn't speak much but we would smile, then look away, feeling a little guilty over the palpable almost painful pleasure that rose through our bodies whenever we sat close together, our accidental touching so filled with sensations that they were indecipherable. We never would have been able to be so alone in the daily routine of our lives. It would have been forbidden to seek out such a time, and we never seemed to have occasion to be so close simply going about the tasks of our young lives, but here in the company of so many adults, when everyone was so attentive to the journey, our time together seemed like solitude. At night I was perplexed that I was often thinking about her instead of anticipating the great moments just ahead when I would see the temple at last, and pray to our God on his very doorstep. But there came a moment I looked back upon many times over the next few years of my life, a moment when Rachael and I, staring effortlessly into each other's eyes, no unease or shyness now, but rather so closely joined that, although they were unspoken, words and sentences and thoughts and feelings were passing back and forth between us as if we were in afternoon discussion at the bazaar. This silent conversation held us, turning strangely painful, almost panicked, as our hands that had unknown to us joined in perfect grip were pulled apart, our families returning to their wagons as we made the last great sweep around a line of hills that would bring us suddenly and imposingly into a position that afforded us our first, indelible view of the temple. I never saw Rachael again; her family moved to Judea within a month of our return and I was told years later that she married a good and devoted man, a clerk who worked with the civil authorities, as did her father. I never forgot her though, and even in the later stages of my human life I thought about her when the pressures and disappointments of my life were hard upon me. But for the moment there was no thought of such things. Each family had returned to its own position in the caravan, the singular identity that had been our nature for the journey returning to the smaller units of households, each huddled together in prayer as we approached the moment the adults knew was soon to come.

And come it did. It was a fantastic sight. With the mid-morning sun reflecting off the gilded walls, the temple was like a mountain of white, when the eye could see past the bright golden fire that reflected from its heights. In all my studies and prayers, my wonder at the beauty of the natural world around me, nothing had prepared me for the grandeur of this sight, because it didn't seem to be of this earth. It looked like a union between heaven and earth, like God's glory coming from above, focused at this point, manifested in a celestial city from which poured a current of power, nourishing and creating as it made it's way down into the lower world. It puzzled me, in fact. As I sat with my family, all our faces turned toward Jerusalem, all kinds of thoughts rushed through my mind. Was God indeed more involved in this world than I had come to believe, did the imperfection and ignorance I had seen all around me as I grew in experience dissipate as one approached this holy spot? Was there earthly perfection here, in stone and precious metal, and would the human custodians of this place also hold the clear reflection of truth as vehicles of the True Word of God?

The perception of transcendent glory hardly diminished as we grew nearer, but it became evident that the temple, as glorious as it had appeared from the distance, was of earthly nature. It was surrounded by solid walls showing a simple, massive face, adorned only by the splendour of its size and pure white color, and by the towers that showed its other nature as a fortress. The walls were uninterrupted in their great smooth length except by the massive gates and heavy brass doors. I don't need to linger on the temple—it has been well described—but I want to explain the impact it had on me as a boy on the verge of manhood. I wanted the temple and all it stood for to be a holy place. I knew it had the blessing of the creator himself. Theoretically it could house a clear and accurate source of truth, a sanctuary for a confused and violent world, a literal fountain of spiritual knowledge. The temple had the potential to nourish first the Jews and later all the world during the dark hours of time as the massive conflict between two spiritual opposites ground its way toward resolution. It was the birthright of a chosen people, a people to whom God had extended his hand on all levels, and I had no reason to doubt that the temple stood in absolute similarity to True Reality. Although the ethereal nature of the temple faded into the very physical solidity of stone and wood and polished metal, nothing I saw as we entered the great city made me question this hope, and it was with wholehearted enthusiasm and faith that I approached the God of Israel and His Temple.

Over and above the splendor of the physical building, I was struck by the colourful streams of people who filled it. There were so many, all dressed and adorned in the very best they could manage, and where material lack may have impeded the ability to furnish a resplendent image, polished, clean, and carefully arranged attire made up the difference. We all smiled as our long days of comparative solitude evaporated into an ocean of moving, friendly, humanity. It wasn't until after we had washed and refreshed ourselves to actually make our way through the gate and into the outer courtyard that I noticed the real poor, the beggars and the infirm, and the hawkers busy selling anything that might be needed for offering. We quickly found our lodgings, humble but clean, and within the city gates, which was something even Jerusalem could not provide to all the thousands of visitors that came with Passover.

Magnificent is the best word for the temple. It continued to grow in splendour and size as we entered deeper into its heart. The first day I was overwhelmed, capable of little but to fill my eyes with the majestic images around me. As the festival went on, I adjusted to the grand scale, and although neither the awe nor the sensory joy I was so immersed in diminished, I found myself looking further, deeper. I was looking for something, some connection between the power I felt and the world of my own thoughts. It was hard to find. The prayer and ritual were little different from what I had been used to all my life, except in sheer size, and despite the imposing environment my curiosity had not been satiated, as I had hoped. At the Passover dinner my family formally vested me with the mantle of religious manhood. It was a larger gathering than usual for my parents had invited friends to make the night special. And it was. I always enjoyed the Passover celebrations, they brought out the best in us all, but this night I was the recipient of more than my share of happiness. I was showered with kindness and affection. Gifts and advice were given with equal generosity. But the next day wasn't as different as I had wanted it to be. I wasn't treated any differently, and certainly I had no more opportunity to insert my own will into the daily activities than I had before. In the innocent naivety of youth I thought—and expected others to expect the same—that I would now begin a very new life as a true Son of the Commandment, as young faithful men were called, dedicating myself to our God and taking each and every action with God and His purpose firmly in mind. In fact, little changed. It was not until our travelling party began readying itself for the journey home that I found myself with more than a moment to myself. When I finally did find myself alone and able to do what I wanted, my mind prompted me to take advantage of where I was, the Holy City. Rachel was not to be found, so I headed back toward the temple in serious contemplation and anxious to discover answers I would need before I continued with what was now, officially, my own destiny.

I made my way slowly through the crowd to the temple, walking and thinking, the sun warm and pleasing. I was in no hurry and I wanted to organize my thoughts and questions. I stopped under the covered colonnade that surrounded the large open courtyard. There were people of all types here, mostly clustered in groups and locked in earnest conversation or listening while a self appointed teacher explained an idea or a text that to him had a particular significance. It was easy to involve myself, and although the crowds had thinned with the end of the festival, the men remaining were a more garrulous group than the general crowd of worshippers the day before. With the formalities of the festival over, this was the time to talk. I joined one group after another, listening for a while to get the gist of the conversation then politely interjecting a comment or two, or posing a question to the man or men I thought most likely to have an answer, or at least a response of interest. I soon realized that answers were not that easy to come by; it was far more likely that my questions would lead to wider and wider circles to consider, with only scripture pulling us back to common ground. Time simply disappeared for me, and it was dark before I felt that I had even scratched the surface of the knowledge I wanted to acquire before I returned to Nazareth. This was nothing like home. Here was everything in one spot, learned men obviously raised in the familiar doctrines and traditions, and also Jews in finery unusual to my eye, their nobility present in voice and quality of thought. These imposing men scoffed at pharisaic doctrine as if it were illegitimate, less holy than the teachings of the Princes and Priests of Jerusalem with whom they identified. And here were men who were not Jews, who argued logically and adamantly for theologies as varied as variation itself, and here were men who spoke in quieter tones about revolt and intrigues I was familiar with but had never had the chance to listen to, much less discuss, in such depth and openness.

Some looked at me sharply when I spoke, but soon turned back to the ebb and flow of words, knowing that a twelve year old Hebrew was probably as well trained as any adult of the nations, and certainly formidable in terms of scripture. Scripture was the cornerstone of every subject being discussed within these walls. By the time darkness appeared I had settled in with a group of about ten men, our theme distilling itself for the time being to the question of whether man's role in this world was to struggle and learn, to strive and achieve, or was it to passively place his fate in the hands of God, without thought of a goal or a material measurement of success. I was startled out of my involvement by the darkness and the sudden thought of my parents, but seeing that no one had come to search me out I felt assured that my mother, at least, being fully aware of the responsibilities that come with religious adulthood, would understand that I must be occupied in the pursuit of new understandings about how I should lead my life as a serious and devout man of God. And where else could I do that but here, within these walls and within His presence? So I let my worries slip away, and followed the group as we all moved toward a dining room beneath the cedar ceilings of the colonnade. We ate and talked, until I slipped to the floor, wrapping myself in the soft wool blanket one of my new friends passed to me just moments before I fell into a deep and very contented sleep.

In the morning I awoke with a great eagerness to plunge into the day. I washed and ate with the group of travelers that remained from last night's discussions, and made my way to a more serene spot to pray and meditate. After a mental review of all that was said the day before I realized I wasn't very satisfied with what I had learned. I saw that the ideas and topics that had been talked about, as stimulating and refreshing as the atmosphere had been, were not much different than what we talked about in school, or during the Sabbath afternoons spent with my family and friends. And certainly the lack of consensus was familiar. I had to shake my head when I thought how virtually any subject not fully accepted as canon seemed to have an equal number of equally smart men defending opposite sides of the question. And this wasn't what I wanted; I wanted real wisdom from men who had lived to see the absoluteness of this wisdom, wisdom that I could use to make decisions about how the rest of my life would be conducted. I wasn't going to get this from the arguments of speculation, so I headed deeper into the temple to find a more unified and enlightened source of advice and counsel. I passed, as we had done just days ago, through the crowded courtyard into the smaller and holier area where the men worshipped and the priests made sacrifice. I found a corner away from the crowds and kneeled to pray, then meditate, and then observe. I watched for at least a couple of hours, until I noticed that the flow of activity did divide itself. There were the priests, going about their tasks with sombre certainty, receiving and attending to the larger offerings. They lent each action the importance it held for the family who may have traveled hundreds of miles to express their dedication to God. But I also noticed that discretely, almost strategically, placed throughout the narrow courtyard were several groups of older men who did not appear to be priests, but who, it was equally evident, had a familiarity and comfort with this holy room that could only have come from years of habitual occupation. As I watched I saw that they were reading from scrolls, not continuously focused on their reading as a student would be, anxious to finish and move on to his next assignment, but with great calm and consideration, a few verses or even pages, followed by a predictable time of contemplation and consideration of what they had just read, although, again, it seemed obvious that they were familiar with every word. Occasionally three or four would engage in conversation, usually referring back to and rereading aloud some portion of the text within a page or two of what they had just read. This format was nothing new to me, the elder men of the synagogue often sat and did just so, but there was a difference here. Unlike the elders of Nazareth there was a persistent calm among these men. It would have been unusual to observe the thinkers of my town reading and discussing scripture without the obligatory and frequent escalation of what had been a conversation to a very animated and usually noisy debate, complete with gesture and enthusiasm that skirted the edges of anger.

I quietly moved myself within earshot and sat. I listened for what seemed a long time, a few hours I suppose. I couldn't make out every word, but I did hear enough to know, basically, what they were talking about. It was like cool water on a sore. Although the tumble of words I had sorted through yesterday was important, it had been more effective in eliminating questions than answering them. There was a new clarity today, a focus that brought awareness of what I needed to know and of what I already knew. I knew, for instance, that armed struggle was not the path of a Godly man. Despite the carefully argued rationalizations that had such appeal to our nationalism and our material wishes, there was no real scriptural support for such a path. It was clear that after the destruction of Solomon's temple the Nation that had once existed with the direct support of God would not truly rise again until the end of the gentile times, until the end of the world and the beginning of a new world, and that both the end and the beginning would be brought about by the spiritual power of God himself, from above. No band of sword wielding zealots, no matter how fierce or well intentioned, was to bring this about. I think all truly religious men of my time knew this, but, men being men, it was hard to accept that we, as the true people of God, would remain under the heel of the great and unholy power of Rome. Being able to discuss these things continuously and intensely had rolled what I had learned in my young life into a long band. I saw what I knew and I saw what I did not know, and here, as I approached one of the circles of wise men, feeling the palpable presence of consciousness that surrounded them like a soft rain, I knew I could learn what I still needed to know.

It was late afternoon by the time I made my first comment to this learned group. I received some long and penetrating glances from a few of these bearded and robed mountains, but no one appeared surprised or provoked by my now immediate presence. I summoned my courage and asked a question that related to the topic they had been discussing for over an hour. I received a reply that seemed to continue with the nature and direction of their conversation, and with that comfort and unspoken acceptance I sat back, figuratively, within myself, and breathed a sigh of relief and pleasure, preparing myself to try and shape this lofty conversation into the form of the Teacher I needed.

It seemed as if only a few minutes had gone by when the words simply ceased. There was prayer, and then our collective attention went to the priests and the altar. It was a sudden reminder of the great and wonderful dream of which I was a part, my eyes lifted up to the huge mass of unhewn stones that formed the alter and beyond to the great height of the face of the holy house, adorned with gold and carved shapes, where even now, as flame and smoke and glorious music rose in sacred unison, the priests dissolved behind the curtained entrance to the most holy, bringing the day of sacrifice to a solemn close. I sat and allowed my body and mind to absorb as much of this sensory feast as I could, and gave my own burning thanks to a God who filled my heart as much as he filled the universe around me. Almost involuntarily my body rose and moved into the outer courtyards, where I talked and ate and slept in a light-filled trance, falling off to sleep as candlelight flickered around me and the soft rise and fall of human voices soothed me to sleep as gently and effectively as my mother's arms.

The morning, however, was bright and clear, and although the images of yesterday's pageantry tried to show themselves as dreams, I knew they were not, and I was soon clean, and filled with enough food and enthusiasm to walk to the alter of Jehovah for the morning sacrifice.

I found the same group assembled as if they had not moved at all, and when I sat, as I had done the day before, several of the men, those closest to me, greeted me by name, with kindness and even affection. Soon we were once again a little universe of our own, plotting our informal but definite course across the immense backdrop of truth and knowledge. But this day was slightly different, tracking a wider circle than the one we traversed the day before. I'm going to quote little scripture. I'm not going to explain why, except to add that no man should think of himself as wise unless he has the knowledge that reveals itself to those who are willing to spend the time to become familiar with and learned in the Word of God. All the conversations I listened to or joined in during the days I now describe were wound around the sacred writings. As I mentioned before, I was becoming comfortable and encouraged that what I had learned over the course of my life about the Word was reasonably complete, and consonant with the foundations and conclusions agreed upon by the elders with whom I now sat, some of who, I now realized, actually were priests. We all agreed that we, the Jews, were in a tough spot. We were alone in a world that was fundamentally dark, spiritually divided and distorted, and inherently without the ability to extract itself from a degraded and violent reality. But we also agreed that the creator had assured us that escape was not only possible but certain, and would come from the hand of the universe itself, from the hand of divine will, not human.

And so, while not suggesting that a few verses can substitute for the formal study of scripture, I noticed that the heart of Truth could be distilled into a relatively small number of key passages if one had absorbed and understood the overall context.

This day we focused on the keystones of our sacred written heritage, and we agreed. We agreed that a day of deliverance, a day of final judgment and ultimate peace, with transcendence over death a part of that peace, was to come to the world. It was also agreed by these keepers of the temple, that this Day of God was literal, and that It would not come before the appearance of the Messiah, the prophesied saviour of the Jews and of the world, and that this appearance was to occur in Israel, and soon. I was surprised that these men were in anticipation of the arrival of the saviour even as we spoke, and I was pleased and surprised that most of these men held that whatever force was to be used to restore the Kingdom of God was going to be spiritual in nature and would be wielded in God's name by the Messiah and His Heavenly Army alone. Mankind would be a passive recipient of this great transformation.

It was to these topics that I tried to steer the discussion in the courtyard, and I found little resistance, in fact it was around the plight and expectations of the children of God that my wise friends seemed most inclined to talk. But there was also a peripheral aspect of our discussions that gave me equal substance to think about over the next few years. I noticed that when we followed the scriptures to their heart concerning what really was to happen in our lifetimes and the life of mankind itself, the harmonious unity of thought that was so powerful and pleasant began to fray. When I asked in the precociousness of youth for more specific details about who and when and where this messiah was to manifest himself, or when I wondered how the divergences between the temple priests and the teachings of the synagogues could be resolved, or why the name of God was apparent in fewer of the scrolls used at the temple than in the villages, I was often surprised to find myself sitting quietly while three or four of my mentors argued points and theories less and less relevant to the scriptures and more and more subjective, and in tones and manners much more similar to the bickering that had puzzled me in the gates and markets of Nazareth. It was just after one such minor disagreement, the faces and the voices returning to more loving countenance and reasoned tones, that I heard the voice of my father at my shoulder. Whatever was left of my dreamlike state vanished as I looked up, and in an instant I saw that my belief I was following the path expected of a young man now dedicated to his God was not shared by Joseph. It seemed only a moment until I was before my mother, standing just outside the entrance that denied her access to the altar, and explaining to her that I honestly had been doing what I thought I should.

On some level I know she agreed with me, and very little was said as we made our way back to the small party that had turned around from its path home, to find me. No one was really angry, but I learned another subtlety of the melding of the law with life. Although I was now an individual, responsible for my thoughts and actions, I was still very much a part of the family, and due to my age, I had to respect my parents' wishes when it came to my whereabouts and activities.

# CHAPTER FOUR

I was glad to get home, but the sheer immenseness of the trip, on every level, made it something that I thought about for a long time. My memories of the temple stayed with me, that first sight of it shining like a white and gold mountain fit so seamlessly with what I imagined God's point of contact with the earth would be like that in a way it became a timeless image, a glimpse of a time to come.

In my mind I went over and over the conversations with the men of the temple courtyard. I could remember virtually every word, the subjects and sequences of the dialogues seeming almost predictable as we slid back and forth along the well-measured landscape of our faith. Although I was familiar with most of the references we used as architecture for our thoughts and words, I had made a few mental notes to study the more esoteric references made by the older men, references that showed a depth of understanding and familiarity with scripture that was obviously more evolved than even the most learned of the local wise men. Especially in Daniel, Ezekiel, and Isaiah I had been given a glimpse of prophetic meaning that had not been evident to me in our local studies. And so with this scholastic catching up to do and feeling the welcome burden of the higher expectations my family and community now had for me as a young adult, the next few years passed happily and productively. By the time I was fourteen, or certainly fifteen, I really was a help to my father, and I could only smile at myself for having thought I always had been. We both worked hard. I loved the work, perhaps even more now that I produced things that translated into real value for my family. The satisfaction I had knowing that we prospered, in a very simple and limited way, true, but prospered none the less, not insignificantly due to my own efforts, allowed me freedom to enjoy myself in other ways when the time I had was undisputedly my own and well deserved. I felt sorrow for others who did not have this simple source of happiness, the joy that came from a loving family and worthwhile work and simple faith, but I knew, even at fifteen, that the deep malignancy of this world was ruthless in the things it denied many of its people, so often taking away the opportunity for happiness even before they knew they had it. But I had it and I knew it, and my perfect instincts kept me from making mistakes that could have ruined it.

I would walk into the nearby hills late in the afternoon and fill myself with pleasure, not often ecstasy, but pleasure. It was so beautiful there. The desert flowers supplied the nose with scents that often made the mouth burst out in appreciation, and the twilight, as it wrapped you and the world around you in a blanket of color and feeling that made you one, was magic. This alchemy was a residue of the presence of God, not some lower occult that sprang from, and led to, emptiness. I had a lot of simple pleasures and busy days, and they easily rolled themselves into months and years.

When I returned to Nazareth from the Passover at Jerusalem I was a boy, despite the fact that I had been formally initiated into manhood, but over the next few years I grew into the world of physical manhood. By fifteen I was tall, and by fifteen I was interested in girls, especially the girls who were turning into women just as I was a man. Among my people the pull of the flesh was not something young adults had to deal with on their own. Everyone talked about it, in fact everyone delighted in talking about it. By about fourteen a boy's mother would begin to plague him about it. 'What do you think about young Sarah, my cousin's girl, isn't she wonderful?' 'Remember son, a good wife is a rare treasure, you should think about that.' 'How will you ever get a good wife if you behave like that, do you want to end up lonely and childless like your uncle Judah?' and fathers were not much better. 'Don't be deceived by a pretty face, my boy, that will fade soon enough and all you will be left with is a sharp and bitter tongue.' 'Don't be too anxious to marry, I can tell you these are the best years for you.' Of course, as new adults, most of us liked the attention, and the topic, as much as we squirmed and shook our heads. But we thought about it too, and by the age when we were beginning to assist in the duties of the synagogue we sometimes found ourselves staring a little too long at some pretty face, or being suddenly entranced by the happy voice of an excited girl talking much longer than expected about something that all at once seemed much more worthy of consideration, even though we didn't really understand or care exactly what it was she was talking about. It was very interesting.

I know I've said this before—and it is no accident I say it again—it was God that was important to us. We had learned and accepted this from the time we were barely talking and it was easy to accept because we saw this faith being worked out by our parents and our neighbors and our town and our nation. Despite the hardships imposed by the outside world, it was easy to see that this truth was real indeed. It worked. It nurtured and protected us, it gave us joy and it gave us strength. And although the rulers of our faith sometimes made it hard not to resist, even resent, the sometimes harsh restraints and unwanted interference or the petty judgments that caused doubt and even pain, the common man knew his faith was good, and that despite the often apparent faults, there was an underlying power and truth to our religion that we never forgot.

So the young had little confusion about love and marriage. We knew we would have both. We thought about it and planned for it. We anticipated, and were often impatient for, the fulfillment of our passions, but we also knew we had to do it correctly or suffer. We were under no illusions that love was the single transcendent ingredient needed for happiness. We knew that love and marriage were part of the fabric of our faith, and simply a stone, a cornerstone yes, but just one stone in the structure that was our life. Like every town Nazareth had its all too visible examples of human tragedy, be it caused by selfish male opportunism or foolish female disregard. Our ability to be patient with our hearts, our ability to avoid mistakes, was made possible by the fact that we simply were not given the chance to make mistakes, or to act impulsively. By the age of puberty boys and girls were not allowed to be alone together. Our parents were not only good at telling us why and when and if, they also watched us like hawks. My moments of emotional and mental intimacy with Rachael came amid a crowd, and if they had been fully noticed by one of the adults we would have been deftly, but kindly, separated, or at least joined in our reverie by an elder.

So I went along with the tide, not making any decisions or drawing any conclusions about romance. After the shock of being told she was gone, I thought about Rachael a lot, and I felt pain at her absence, but by the time I was fifteen she seemed to cross my mind only on rare occasions, and when she did I felt more warmth than pain. I was in no hurry to replace her with another, although I did wish I might find myself gazing into eyes as captivating as hers, by simple circumstance or coincidence. But I had another area of interest.

As I mentioned, I got great enjoyment from walking in the quiet places. By the time I was eighteen or so I knew the land around Nazareth so well I could walk for miles without ever having to wonder where I was going. And so I never had to hurry. I could sit and look. I could close my eyes and breathe, and open them again to smile at the beauty around me.

God was certainly present, but in a quiet and subtle way. I never had much in the way of adventure, spiritually or otherwise, but I had a gentle peace that bound the daily activities of my life into a slowly filling awareness. By the time I was in my early twenties I felt big. I was full grown, and I appreciated my strength and my feeling of comfort with my world. My time alone left me practiced at meditation, and the confines of contemplation began to yield a deeper and brighter light, one that brought with it a vague restlessness. More and more when I made my way home after an afternoon or evening in the hills, I noticed a curious division of perception. There was a surface layer I saw with my senses that seemed complete and smooth and fully in harmony with my thoughts and my concepts of what life was, but I often found myself startled by how this surface cracked when I engaged in physical contact with things that apparently had a deeper will of their own. A leather bag or a piece of food could suddenly appear separate, foreign even, to my touch and sight, causing me to draw back and find myself in a slightly different world, separate and fragmented, small and sharp, where an instant before it had been whole and vast. This feeling was most evident when someone spoke to me, or when I listened to the conversation of others as I rejoined my village. Sometimes this feeling was so strong that when a friend or even a family member spoke to me their words and the resulting ripples of meaning that penetrated my own surprisingly delicate fabric of reality would almost feel like an assault on the invisible cords of feeling within me, and I would have to look away, smiling to disguise the unexpected effects of their simple comments. I gave up trying to protect this fragile calm that came from isolation. There was no way to avoid natural contact with people, or things for that matter, that obviously had no inherent malice toward me. They were simply my life, but I was surprised at how separate the world could be from my own internal peace.

I was twenty-four when my father died. It was sudden and it shocked us all. By this time I had four brothers and two sisters, and we all took for granted and depended on the quiet goodness of Joseph. All men mourn so I have little to say about the months after his death. As the oldest I had to place my sorrow behind the unexpected responsibilities I now had. I didn't have to think about changing, I simply changed. I embraced my mother with all my strength and faith. I held my brothers and sisters with newfound force, keeping the empty spaces filled with work and prayer, and trying to allow our tears to merge and lose themselves in the long history of sorrow we held as a people. We had faith, and the deep wisdom and hitherto untapped strength of my mother gave solace and peace to us all.

Any unborn thoughts I may have had about my growing curiosity and restlessness concerning my future disappeared. I took over the workshop and the tasks that went along with having to see that our family would not suffer materially. I journeyed to the villages and merchants that had supplied my father with wood and to the markets and families that bought what we made. I learned to talk and bargain, to sit with the men at the gates and eat and drink, not just for the joy of discussing our faith and our future, but knowing that at the end of the day I could expect old customers to clasp my arm and offer their fraternity to a new family head, a man like them, with a silent oath of shared needs and burdens. Long walks with their accompanying questions about the nature of what was and what was to come became rare for the first few years after Joseph passed. As the pain subsided I allowed myself more freedom, and I began to return to some of my old solitudes, surprised to find a familiar cave or cluster of trees unchanged in its ability to offer shade and the sweet light of spiritual retreat.

Once again I sought time alone in prayer and meditation and

simple idyll, and I found the separation between the world of my aloneness and the world of my role as a man was more distinct than ever. It no longer shocked me to find the bright, singing universe I carried with me as I walked toward the village knocked and buffeted into a resigned but familiar normality. But this difference led me to look forward all the more to the times I had by myself. My study had progressed, and the puzzlement and wonder I once held at the depth of scriptural knowledge displayed by the wise teachers at the temple so long ago had been replaced by simple appreciation for the power and wisdom of the holy texts. It was this wisdom that formed the basis of my meditation. I had found the thread of secrets that circles its way through the Word of God, and I was more and more in anticipation of what was to come. I didn't think of myself as unique or special, but I knew how special mankind inherently was. I saw that the revealing of that potential was something to come, prophesied by men of the past and demanding of men of the present, and I looked forward to making my contribution to that revelation of our divine nature. I had learned from men, both historical and contemporary. Even in Nazareth there were men, unheralded and seemingly unlikely men, who had come to see a hidden depth to the world of the senses, and who had slipped away from the benefits of prominence to the hidden rewards of introspection and dedication to the search for a conscious awareness of the Living God. I had made a point of sitting and talking to these men. They all shared a certain excitement about the times we lived in, certain that great things were going to happen, and eager to share their certainty. It reinvigorated them to pass on what they knew or thought. I knew something was going on beneath the surface, but I had no inclination to withdraw from daily life. At twenty-eight I had clear obligations, and whatever Truth had in store, it lay enfolded in the fact that my family needed me.

Sarah and I knew each other, being children of families that had slightly intersecting orbits, but it seemed we met for the first time on a day preceding the Sabbath, late in the afternoon as I made my way back to my family to prepare for the evening meal. I was happy, and filled with the spirit of my own world when I saw her, undoubtedly on her way home as I was. As we approached our eyes met and she spoke my name in polite greeting. She was smiling, and I realized there were no sharp corners to the sound of her voice or the wave of her thoughts. In fact I felt a familiarity with the sound and quality of her voice that belied the depth of our relationship. We just smiled at each other, with no inclination to avert our eyes or stop the motion of the shared spirit that grew, and kept growing, between us. I saw Rachael in her face, and then herself, Sarah. I know I should have been self-conscious about the joy I was feeling at the nearness and intensity of her beauty, but whatever reticence I might have had was swept away in the force of the feeling. We just stared, until her face was framed in light and I looked away. Her name finally escaped my lips, and I reached for her hand. We walked silently for a few steps, until the approaching darkness reminded us that we had to go. To say that I was content as I walked the short distance to my home would be an understatement. My immediate future seemed clear as I tried to sort out the blaze of emotions that occupied my mind and heart. My responsibility to my family could not be ignored, and if I was to remain here in Nazareth to look after my mother and my younger siblings it seemed only natural and fitting that I be married. And at that moment I wanted nothing else.

The next morning I told my mother about Sarah. She was smiling and very attentive as I tried to explain my new feelings. I don't recall what she said, but I know she was bursting with happiness when she hugged me and assured me that she knew exactly how to proceed. It was not long before I found myself at Sarah's family's table, eating and joining in the rather festive mood of the meal, enjoying the curious glances of her sisters, and feeling a kind of pride that they seemed so pleased with our new interest in each other.

The next few months went happily and predictably. Since Sarah and I were older than most of the young people who displayed the symptoms of romance, we were pretty much left alone to get to know each other at our own pace. Both families knew we were loyal to our beliefs, and no one, including ourselves, had any fears about our ability to control our rather evident passion.

Sarah was everything I could have wanted. She was as beautiful as her namesake, and as striking for her calm confidence and spiritual strength as for her beauty. I took her with me on walks to the more accessible and inspiring of my rural haunts, and we spent as much time as we could talking about the things that were important to us, and enjoying the shear magnitude of what we had, not too surprisingly, in common.

I suppose we would have married within a year or two. But it just happened. We were talking, as we always seemed to be, words and thoughts flowing along lines as parallel as the tracks of a cart, when we suddenly found ourselves silent. Sarah knew the word of God. I wasn't surprised by her knowledge, knowing her family and our traditions, but it was a source of great joy for me that she could speak so clearly about our faith, and share with me the subtleties of truth in a way I found faultless. Perhaps that is why I was so surprised at our impasse. I had been speaking about our life, and about my enthusiasm for a future certain to be filled with the mystery and power of God, and about how I looked forward to a time when our world would be replaced by the True Reality, a reality that would show our present life to be the shadow that it is. I suppose, in retrospect, I had never spoken this way to anyone, and although the thought was a common one to me, it had always been confined to internal dialogue. Even though everything I said was true, I can see it seemed unreal and a little ungrounded. But be it due to destiny or over zealousness or lack of context, for us it was not well said. Even after I had rephrased my comments we were no closer to agreement. "What is so wrong with the world we have, Jesus," she said. "I know that our world isn't perfect, but we need to have faith in God, and if we're good, things will work out." I calmed myself and grew more serious. "Sarah, I know that this world holds a lot of beauty, and that happiness is a thing to be sought after, but doesn't God make it clear in scripture that it is in a 'new' world that we will find peace?" "But it's not up to us, Jesus, to make that happen…" and so it went. I tried my best to explain to her that I agreed with her, but, for honesty's sake I had to add that although faith was necessary and good, like the prophets before us a man had to be willing to do what God required in order to make a contribution to the unfolding of His will upon this earth, even if that meant sacrifice. Soon she was silent. I could see disbelief in her mind. I watched as she thought about her children yet to come, and how she recoiled at the image of a husband who might put them all in danger simply for the sake of speaking out, of making a fuss. I felt joy leave my body. I couldn't believe it. Here, invading this most cherished of moments, was the same old shard of separation that had disrupted my sense of oneness so many times before. Here, in the intimacy of a bond I had been so comfortable with, in a love that felt so natural and good that our closeness should have lasted forever, was a giant rift. It seemed unfair to me that we had been brought together by circumstance and common intention, by destiny it seemed, only to arrive at this subtle but fiercely immovable difference of opinion. As we left each other that day, awkwardly but hopeful tomorrow would set things straight, I started to face something I had ignored for a long time. Perhaps the obedience I felt to God was not shared by the natural direction of my life. I had always managed an uneasy truce between memories of my mother's words telling of a Sacred Heritage, a Kingship from the house of David, and the daily reality of my life, a truce that allowed perhaps that those ideas were simply metaphorical, and would reveal themselves as symbols of spiritual goals pursued and gained. But war had come to that previously unchallenged peace. I felt an unwanted certainty grow within me that adherence to what I saw so clearly as the right thing to do, following the will of God, was going to move me further and further apart from the path I would have chosen if I concerned myself only with the needs of the physical man. This contradicted the assumption I previously held that I lived in a world where doing the right thing materially was synonymous with doing the right thing spiritually. Of course such harmony is how it should be in the world, how we try to make it, even how it is for some men some times. But the true source of pain for all men is that we are separated from such integration, regardless of how well we behave or how lucky we are.

I know that it may seem strange to hear about this incident, on such a personal level, when there is no hint of it in scripture. But it is important to know why I never married. Within a few days of our uneasy parting, I knew I could never marry. It simply would be unfair, to any woman, because of the pain I now knew my life would bring to her. I thought I understood, in a broad sense, what my life required of me, but no human could see the path I had to walk without a perfect nature of their own, and even Sarah did not have that capability. She would have been torn apart by conflict and doubt over what was to happen, unsure of herself and unsure of me, a victim of agonies that were unnecessary if I simply bore them myself, substituting solitude for solace. It was this dawning awareness that brought me the deepest pain of my life, for, from the moment of this realization, I was alone. I was always alone. I had no hesitation, in fact I embraced the idea that I redefine the conflict between comfort and faith, if faith required this, but there was a terrible sickness of heart knowing that I could never ask this sacrifice from someone who would become one with me in flesh.

But I knew what to do, and I knew without insecurity, that this was what to do, and so the pain became simply a part of my life, like a handicap that I bore but didn't dwell upon again.

I could ask for love from the position of teacher and friend, and accept love as a teacher and friend, but I could never subject a woman to physical union when the inevitable pain would fall so unevenly on her.

It seems now like a good moment to explain a little of how my mind saw the world at that time. I had no real awareness in terms of understandable images of who I was or what was to come. I was growing. I functioned perfectly, and thus I had had no real reason to manifest what I knew in words or thoughts. The mind is the part of the body that joins the physical with the spiritual. Working properly, it does the bidding of the individual spirit of each man. It connects the spirit to the physical body. If spirit is silenced or subverted, the mind operates the body based on what it has learned to that point, unable to take advantage of new spiritual intuition, and so unable to avoid error. Each man has spirit that is confined to his own body; it belongs to him and allows him to operate as a creature of both the seen and unseen worlds. Being of the same nature as the spirit of God, the spirit of each man has the capability, through the oneness of all spirit, to take direction, knowledge, and strength from the spirit of the universe, and thus thrive in the world of time and space.

So when I observed the world I had knowledge through spirit of what I saw and what it meant, what it was, and what was to come, but this knowledge did not become thought until it needed to, or until I directed my conscious inquiry toward it. A simple example may be understandable. When I looked at someone, I saw them. But I more than saw them: I could also feel their condition. I did not think about it, but in my vision I saw and understood any part of their spirit that was not in harmony with the spirit of the universe around them. Most of the time this difference was not brought into awareness, for all men had separation from the perfect spirit, so to my sight it was simply a man or a woman. But if this aberration was large enough or strong enough it would stand out and catch my attention. I knew what it was even as I looked, and if I focused, the knowledge that existed in spirit would translate, through the mind, into thought and then symbols, as words. The words might be pain, or anger, or confusion, or hatred, but they brought to consciousness a knowledge already shared by my spirit and the spirit of the universe. We all operate like this, and I know many of you know this, but the point I want to make is that I did not know in a verbal, cerebral sense, at this time of my life, what was to happen in the future, or even what was happening in the moment. But I did have a silent knowledge, knowledge in light you might say, of both, and I rested in and relied on that consciousness, that faith which is present in the silence of perception.

Within a month of my realization that marriage was not a possibility, my attention shifted to what that meant, and spirit began to bring the answer into awareness. As the awareness grew it subtly altered the reality around me. I looked upon my family and I saw that things had changed. Time had healed the wounds of Joseph's death as much as such wounds heal, and two of my brothers had grown to mature men. If I envisioned them without me, I saw that they would be perfectly able to look after my mother and my sisters. This was a bit of a surprise, because I had felt such a burden of responsibility for them all, and although I had looked forward to this responsibility, I now saw that my life was not going to unfold as I had expected. I knew my mother was distraught as the realization that I was not going to marry Sarah sunk in, for she shared the question of what my future held, and now she was worried.

Things went along normally for a while, but one day, as spring approached, my mother drew me aside, asking me to sit with her in the warm sun of the early afternoon. "You know your cousin has been preaching in the desert, Jesus, and now he is at the river Jordan. Everyone is talking about him; he is drawing people from the cities and calling for us all to repent, because the events of heaven are revealing themselves. What do you think about what he is doing?" I stalled a little; I wasn't ready to relate what John was doing to my own life. She persevered and I answered, surprised a little by my own words. She looked at me in silence, and then said in a voice that allowed no doubt, "Go Jesus, go to him, begin what you were born to do, I have done all I can." By the end of summer I was gone.

There were no tears. There was apprehension, there was love, and there was a feeling of charged fullness like the pressure of an approaching desert storm, but there were no tears.

# CHAPTER FIVE

I took very little with me. I walked east along the ridge of hills, and by nightfall I was in land that was unfamiliar, although I knew it would lead down into the valley that skirted the hills, and would wind south and east toward the Jordan.

In the morning it seemed as if I was a different person. I had no thoughts of the past. As I looked at my arms and legs I felt a sense of seeing things for the first time. Inside I was the same. I mean the overall texture of my nature seemed the same, but the world was different. The vastness of the horizon seemed more immediate, and my vision based its images more on light than on form, and with that came a blurring of the lines between my own body and the world around me. I was intensely alive, and yet strangely light, seeming almost to flow rather than walk. This feeling diminished as time passed. Sometimes the exertion of a climb and the heat it brought with it sharpened the foreground and made my body more substantial, sharpening the feeling and color of my clothing, my skin, as if I had gained in density and mass. Sometimes the feeling of the staff in my hand held my attention just beneath the effort of searching ahead for the path. What had been inert as a piece of wood was now charged with energy, seeming to change back and forth from being almost weightless to a heavy solidity that pulled and pointed in one direction or another as if attached to the world around it by an invisible force. I was not unfamiliar with any of these sensations, but they were exaggerated from anything I had felt before, and had a new feeling of importance, of urgency.

I didn't feel as if I wanted to see anyone right away, until I felt comfortable with myself, and more certain of what I was doing, so I took a long time to reach the river. I spent more and more time sitting and thinking, watching the world as my thoughts played in and out of my mind. What was I doing? I finally asked myself that question in very deliberate words.

I thought about my life, much as I have outlined it here. I prayed. I waited. I thought, and I prayed again. After a while I saw the pattern. I went back and forth over the events that rose in my memory until nothing new interjected itself to interrupt the overall view. I didn't know why I should be different than anyone else, but I also realized no one knows why he or she is confined within themselves, separate. I knew there was a God. I knew there was a world beyond our own and greater than our own. I knew a time would come when that greater world would impose itself upon the earth and require us to harmonize with a reality that reflected the true nature of God. I knew we waited for this. I knew there was a role for me to play in this, and when I was really honest with myself I knew it was to be a role that would bring me close to God and to His Will.

As I rose from this conclusive meditation, the final thoughts were still speaking, forming. I had to accept my path, I had to embrace it, and I vowed, even as I reached for my pack and continued down toward the area where I expected John to be, to embrace it fully and not to look back.

The force of my resolve brought about enthusiasm, and I smiled, a little foolishly as men do when they surrender themselves to the living God and feel the warmth of his acceptance and approval. I walked slowly now, letting the fullness and beauty of each moment rise and fall in body, mind, and heart. Even though no one was watching, out of some sense of natural decorum I consciously urged the smile to leave my lips and express itself only in my eyes and mind.

I walked south, along the western bank of the Jordan, sometimes winding up into the hills so that the river was out of sight, but always my path returned within sight of the water. After some time I crossed the river at a spot that I could see would be relatively easy. I knew from local gossip that John had been preaching in the country around the river, and that on the eastern side, a few days walk from the sea of Galilee, he had settled in, baptizing Jews in large numbers as they poured out from Judea and Galilee to hear his message, a message that was resonating with the people of Israel, causing much speculation as to who this man was, and what, if anything, his dramatic rise to prominence meant.

I hadn't seen my cousin for almost twenty years. I suspect that my mother in some way had something to do with that. The dramatic events that occurred at the time John and I were born weighed invisibly, but heavily, over both Mary and Elizabeth. It wasn't until I knew I was leaving Nazareth that my mother and I even discussed the prophecies made concerning John when he was born. I am sure it was the disconcertingly consistent way in which the predictions were now playing out that made her draw on her deepest memories, to relive and remind me of the time in her life when she was visited by angels. It had been a time when faith and love and life had been imposed against the brilliant light of eternity. The spirit of God had made itself known to her, and the result of that transcendent union had yielded my life. It had been difficult for her to believe that the angel Gabriel really was the angel Gabriel when he spoke to her, but the truth speaks in a fair language. There have always been some who can recognize the speech of the universal tongue, for that part of us which is from God, knows God. But to accept into full awareness the fact that you are to be mother to the Son of God, a man destined to rule over all Israel in a supernatural fashion, is beyond the ability of any mortal, and it was spirit that held my mother free from any conflicts of mind and spirit, as befit the purity and power and dignity of the things that had taken place. But the dramatic intensity of the events surrounding my birth some 30 years before had been short lived. By the time I was five, Life had become life for my mother, and spectral words and thoughts, even holy ones, are by nature rare, and soon loose their solidity in the progress of time. So it was with her.

But now there was John. I have spoken about John before, but I want to elaborate a little, in the same way I was rethinking these matters as I walked toward our reunion. Elizabeth and Mary were separated by years, Elizabeth being the elder, and in their youth, the more ascendant of the two. Although raised together in the extended family, Elizabeth's parents were wealthy and prominent, being rich in faith as well as earthly goods. Elizabeth and Mary loved each other, a kindred affection based perhaps on the sincerity of faith common to both girls, and she and my mother were inseparable. Consequently the girls were educated together, Mary benefiting from the high training Elizabeth required to fulfill her parents' desire that she marry a righteous and influential man. The intensity of their religious training went well with both women, and they shared a faith and passion that held the admiration of all they met. They were both dedicated to the God of Israel with the full force of their joy and power, as well as with their considerable beauty and intelligence. Marriage would only be a deeper commitment to their religion and the truth, for in our traditions, asceticism, especially for a woman, was the path of the weak, not the strong.

It was an intense time for them, their faith playing out in that uncommon earthly occurrence where the confluences of earth and spirit come together, and great Work is done. They felt this, and the bond between them became a spiritual one, sisters approaching the bright throne of eternity, walking hand in hand, excited and filled with joy, as their path spiralled ever closer to the golden center.

Auspicious event followed auspicious event, and when Elizabeth married Zechariah, an older man, a respected and admired priest, a handsome man, it seemed earth and heaven were one for her, for she loved him almost as intensely as her faith.

The marriage tested their relationship, of course, but Mary was able to live with the new household for quite a long time, and the new role Elizabeth adopted as wife had plenty of room for female companionship and shared duties. But Elizabeth was getting older, by childbearing standards, and still no child had come, and it appeared she was barren. Although unspoken, this was a terrible strain, casting a communal doubt on her relationship with God, that He not favor her with the child both families so desired, and expected. None the less, both women remained strong in faith and strong in friendship, certain that the spirit of life was real in their lives, incapable of fostering anything but the will of the creator.

It wasn't until Mary, now in her twenties, was betrothed to Joseph, an upright and faithful man, but poor compared to the upper echelons of the priesthood that Zechariah occupied, that a real separation occurred. Mary would go to live in Nazareth; Elizabeth would remain in more noble dwellings, in Judea.

They prayed and held each other, weeping, promising never to let anything come between their sacred friendship, but knowing they would slip further and further from each other as the currents of their disparate futures moved on.

It seemed their shared vision of spiritual fulfillment would fade into good, but different, separate and more mundane lives. But they were determined, and within a year of their separation, held together in prayer and faith, both were rewarded in ways that come

63

seldom, even to the most persevering of seekers.

No more than the most fortunate of men have direct contact with spiritual beings in their mortal lives, for this only occurs when it is necessary in some way for the outworking of this world's tragic path to deliverance. And fortunate were both Mary and Elizabeth. We know what happened. John's birth was predicted and proclaimed by Gabriel, who both named him and promised that he was to be a man great in the eyes of God, with the power and spirit of Elijah to turn the hearts of men back to God. And then there were the even more far reaching and absolute prophecies about me. Every possible dream of both Mary and Elizabeth was realized by the time of my birth, but these realizations proved the beginning of the end for the almost dreamlike years of intensity, faith, and spirit they had shared. My mother's visit to Elizabeth in her sixth month of pregnancy signalled a triumphant end to the time of their great sisterhood, and they moved with great happiness into a future that portended to be more than even they could have imagined.

Their lives proceeded with nothing to suggest that the future held less than had been foretold, but as the years passed without any real impact or influence from the miracles, their need for such catastrophic underpinnings also diminished. Neither woman was the type to boast or remind others of what had happened, and as their children grew the events of the past took on an almost academic tone. But for Elizabeth this did not mean she did not use the past as an incentive for John to excel, for both she and her husband were of the priesthood, Elizabeth a direct descendant of the house of Aaron, and Zechariah an active priest in the temple of Jehovah. Zechariah had been given instructions directly from Gabriel as to how to raise John, and the nature of his future, and since the verity of the angel's words had been punctuated by blindness until the child's birth, a reminder that a priest should not doubt his faith, both parents brought John up to take his place as a prophet of God. They did not fully appreciate the way John manifested his destiny, choosing the desert rather than the temple, choosing ascetic purity to tradition, and offending many with his direct and relentlessly serious nature. John, in fact, had become a worry to his parents by the time of his late adolescence, rejecting the formality and security of the temple, preferring to spend long periods of time in the desert, fasting and having little to do with the affairs of men. He was charismatic and engaging, but in the way that brings parents a little more concern than contentment. But John was progressing in the training of a priest, and that satisfied them, at least until he was thirty. It was then expected that he take up his post at the temple as a novice priest, but instead John returned to the desert and began to rail against both the people of Israel and their Priesthood.

It wasn't until the word had spread that John was preaching with an intensity that recalled old miracles, attracting multitudes of, first curious then repentant, Jews into the wild desert, that mother began to see that another chapter was opening. She knew all to well that the 'One' John talked about coming behind him was me, and if that was true, so was the immensity of what lay ahead. And so it was that she told me everything she knew, every word, every astonishing event that concerned either John or me, and sent me out to meet him, and my destiny.

And now I was looking down on a scene that seemed to strand me in time; as if I had stood on that very spot for an eternity.

It was a place where the water of the Jordan spilled out into the desert, down a ravine that was lined with hills, where it joined a large pool created by an underground spring. The northern side of the pool was dense with reeds, but on the south the water formed a small lagoon that stretched up against the soft rounded dunes of the desert. The hills surrounded the area, except for a flat plateau that eased into the water, as if inviting a visitor. At this spot the clear water lapped against the sand and gradually deepened as it joined the even deeper water that filled the gorge leading back to the river. Around the pool there were tents, placed on the tops of the low hills and affording a view of the pool. Those who had come more recently camped behind, so that the area resembled a nomadic campsite.

I had first seen the camp and pool as I came over a rather steep hill and stood at the top. The ground sloped gently down, quite a long distance, to the pool itself. I could see that John was in the water, with a small line of people waiting in the shallows for their call to baptism, and a much larger crowd of people watching the events from the lower hills. I realized that I made a much more dramatic figure than I wanted to, as I stood on the top of the knoll, seeming almost to loom down on the group below, and my feelings of unease increased as I saw John look up toward me, the eyes of the crowd following his in slow unison. The meeting of our respective gazes had an almost palpable effect on me, as if some unseen hand had pushed me to alertness.

We stood immobile for what seemed a long time, John's arms dropping to his side, me leaning on my staff and staring across the distance, allowing the flow of sunlight, water, spirit, and thought to filter through my eyes and mind, until I knew what I must do. One step at a time I began to walk down the hill toward him.

As I said, it was quite a long way, and it seemed that with each step both focus and spirit increased until the moment was pregnant with energy and intensity, our eyes joining in more exact communion as I crossed the void to meet him.

It seemed like a long journey. I had never experienced exactly these sensations. My approach had become an event separate from the cohesive continuum of my life, as if in climbing to the top of a hill and looking out across to the new horizon I had discovered a world completely different from the one I had known. I suppose that is pretty much what was happening. After shaking off the discomfort of suddenly finding myself the object of attention to such a crowd, and realizing that the private, familial meeting I had envisioned was not to be, I resigned myself to the circumstance, opening my heart and mind to God, asking for advice.

I had time to think. Each step held a thought, a question, or an answer. After moving only a few paces, the vista before me became very bright. I saw clearly the crowd of suddenly subdued onlookers blending in with the desert and the water, and the flickering motion of their tents and banners. I saw John, standing motionlessly in the shallow water, his long black hair and curling, chiselled beard framed with light from the sun and water. Other than the quiet ripples of movement from the tents there was no motion or sound, only a fullness, and I knew with certainty, or felt with certainty to be more correct, that all of us were sharing the same moment. We were like a crowd within a single tent, all rapt upon the same actions taking place before us, entirely caught in the enchantment of the extraordinary events that were unfolding.

My discomfort returned, and although I don't think I actually stopped walking, my mind certainly put a halt to what was going on. Why was so much attention on me? Was I playing the prince, or perhaps the prophet? This felt like vanity and posturing. Why did it seem that I could not stop or turn around or simply take a place with the others on the shore? My life had been without fault, and that had been achieved without effort, due to my original nature's freedom from the irremovable dye of imperfection. Pride and the need to be admired had never held the slightest temptation, and yet here it seemed I had engineered, consciously or unconsciously, an opportunity for me to hog the stage.

Answers came quickly, even as my eyes dropped to the ground and then rose to meet the man who stood before me. This was it. The stories that my mother had told me about John, about my birth, about my birthright as the Son of God, these ideas that I had thought about at leisure and when it suited me, could no longer be shuffled off into the confines of memory to be ignored or pulled out for a few minutes of speculation. I had always known they were true, and I had, almost secretly, tried to make sure that I lived up to whatever gift I had been given, but I had never tried with force of choice to bring these mysteries into greater prominence.

I had known for months that my life had to change. This was why my mother had said that it was time to go and see my cousin—John. I remembered now each word she had told me about him as clearly as I recalled everything that had been said about myself. Had it not become clear to me over the last year that if I was to believe in what had been said about me I would have to believe in it all, even the hard part, that God was to give me the throne of David, that I was to rule over all the world in God's name? Was not John to go forth with the spirit of Elijah to prepare the way? If all this was really true, at some point I was going to have to accept It, and become It with my full devotion. It was dawning on me, quickly, that this was that point. I also realized that John had made this moment possible for me. He had started the whole thing rolling when, at God's command, he had irreversibly abandoned tradition and began preaching to Israel to repent, to return to God, to prepare itself, in fact, for me. This was the moment in which all these formerly abstract notions became real. I was at the center of a vortex of energy, spiritual and human, and I had to decide: either drop all pretence of believing that the words said about me were true, turn around and go back to Nazareth, content with my life as a carpenter, or, accept it all, swallow my humility, and move on, accepting that I did indeed have a Grand Destiny.

I had finished these thoughts as my eyes again met John's. I could see that he had been thinking the same thoughts as I. He was remembering the same prophetic words that he had heard as a child. They had been repeated often as he grew up, and he had come to accept them in the full light of truth. He had moved ahead fearlessly with the will of God. And now, here I was. I have never felt such love and gratitude for another man as I did at that instant. John's appearance was almost wild, wild yet striking. He was a paradox of strength and mildness. It was easy to see why he had captured the interest of the nation. His gaze was calm and strong, but filled with nuance and power, and with a certain joy that played around the edge of humor, a word I had never heard used in relation to John. We had met as children several times, but not since we were boys, and the image of the man I saw before me held little resemblance to the shy and withdrawn boy I remembered. I had always liked John; even as a child he had held a pure kind of resolve that I found reassuring, but we had never become close. I think we both knew it had not been time to compare our visions of the future. But now the time had come, and within those first few yards of my approach to the pool we had silently completed the discussion of our related lives. He knew who I was and I knew who he was. He had allowed me to grow in power and knowledge, in relative obscurity, while he began the assault on the world. He had gone to Israel with the message that My arrival had come; that the time had come to give up the expediencies of hypocrisy and weakness, pervasive in the priesthood and the nation alike; that this was the time to remember God and all that he had said; the time to ask for forgiveness and prepare for the approach of the Kingdom of Heaven.

But was I bringing this Kingdom? I suppose it was possible, but that question I cast into the future, and with a new joy welling up within me I left such thoughts and began to make my way toward John with new purpose.

It was as if the remaining 20 yards were the only path that existed.

I sensed and saw, in a fashion just above human vision, a canopy of light, and behind that canopy I knew were eyes, angelic for a certainty.

By the time I did reach John, and clasped his arm, neither of us had words. And then he spoke, words like the strong desert honey he ate, saying, "I need to be baptized by you, and do you come to me?" [2]

I stared at him for a moment before I realized that indeed I did need to be baptized by him, for he had been given it as a sign of what was to occur, and so I replied, with as much kindness as I could, for I somehow knew we would have little time together, "Let it be so now; it is proper for us to do this to fulfill all righteousness." [3] I saw that he agreed, and I made my way up the bank to await my turn.

I turned back toward John when I reached a small dune just out of the reach of the water. The people had returned to themselves, my motion away from John breaking the grip of the previous few minutes. They were looking to each other, mumbling words of conspiratorial amazement, and soon the few who had been awaiting baptism before my sudden intervention on the scene began to make their way to John, who spoke to them and led them in prayer before immersing them in the water. The baptism was not performed as a cleansing of their sins through his authority from God, but as an act of repentance on their part, a request for a sense of right and wrong, and a sign of renewed devotion to their God. I could hear him speak to each one, and though I missed some words I could tell that each message was for that person alone, the tone changing from sympathy to affection, from warning to encouragement, each man receiving an inspired advice, a clue as to how to live his new life. When he had finished his questioning he would ask if the man wished to pray. Some did, but most let him lead them as they approached the heart of the universe to show dedication and renewed submission, and to ask for reconciliation.

Many people made their way to John that afternoon, the power of the events of the day deciding many of the uncertain ones. As the last, a young woman, came out of the pool, I made my way into the water.

The baptism by John, as I have said before, because it is important, was a baptism of repentance, and a rededication to obeying the will of God by adherence to the Law of Moses. Since I had committed no crime under the law, I had nothing to repent, and I wondered why I felt compelled to do this thing. As I stopped before him, captivated once again by the power of his presence and surprised by the way the light of my own being rose to meet his, I began to pray. I addressed my God first by silence, until I found the thought that mirrored the truth of Him. He was all things, the center and living creator of all things past and present, Love and nothing else, capable of nothing but Love. Then, by faith that this thought had brought me close to God, I felt confident to proceed. "I do not know why I take this baptism, Father, but should I refuse to show my dedication to you in any way? No, I approach you in love and gratefulness, asking that you clarify why I am here, and what I am to do. I know that you have blessed me, but of some things I am unclear. I ask that you give me knowledge, so I may serve you according to your will."

As I thought these words, and with my eyes still closed, the great hands of John gripped the sides of my head, the power they held filling my head with a bright golden light. I felt myself being pulled backward as his thumb and finger held my nose against the water. The coolness of the water moved quickly up my back and arms until I felt my head immersed and the waters close over me.

# CHAPTER SIX

---- ℀ ----

God is everywhere.

I was holding that thought as I came up out of the water. God is everywhere. Did the water daze me? No, my mind felt sharp and alive, and indeed I did agree that God was everywhere. The sky above was white, either by cloud or light or both, and I saw blue strips of day bright along the horizon, and the sand was the gold of the desert. My spirit pushed upward toward the clouds and the joy they contained. As I took a breath I was awake, and my eyes returned to the sky.

The clouds broke in the center of the sky and began to fall toward me. Rigid billows edged with gold, grew and curled toward me, gathering speed as if they were new light. When the pouring sky reached me, the force that I braced myself against never came. Instead the clouds, the sky, the light, the heavens themselves passed through me, and into me. And I was left, left in the center of a circle that was the universe. And this universe was I. I knew from meditation that every point in heaven is the center of its own universe, except the throne of God, which is more, and here I was in mine. But it was not like meditation. It was Real. The heavens and the earth were within me. My thoughts were born from celestial motion occurring millions of miles away, and yet they were my thoughts, within me. My size seemed limitless. I moved my arm to see if I still had form, and I watched the arm move through space like a net through water, ripples of force moving out and disappearing. I saw the effect of the motion of my arm, and I saw and felt the ripple of cause that moved out into the circle of the world. I saw with the dreamlike eye of my mind the rise and fall of the new alignment of the universe, changed simply because of one small action by my body. I saw caravans turn to face their destination, women holding their infants up above their heads, smiling up at the little face above them, men on horseback slowly turning their heads toward the east. Everything moved, and then, as the moment passed, settled down like snowflakes to the still silence of my motionless present.

In the center it is static. In the heavens there is no motion that does not originate from God. So if God does not move there is nothing but the brilliant flow of golden light and the ecstasy of the lotus. On this earth, separated from God and heaven by choice, there is a cacophony of motion. But now I held the heavens within me, and since I was the stuff of earth, the kingdom of heaven had indeed come to earth. By the power of heaven I now controlled the motion of the earth. Other men have held this power, but for a fleeting time, and without the purpose and intention of the living God. Even the simple motion of my arm was uniquely in accord with the will of the spirit, which monitors God's will. And the billions upon billions of effects that the motion of my arm created passed through the universe like a warm breeze, joining the millions of other actions taking place at that moment all with the blessing of, and by the will of, God.

The world around me was frozen. The crowd was asleep or in a trance of introspection. John was looking down, for the rush of spirit had come to him as vision in the form of a bird, and then in the form of sound, which said to him, "This is my Son, whom I love; with him I am well pleased."[4]

I thought before I moved, for I guessed, after viewing the tide of causation that the motion of my arm had caused, what a turbulence would begin when I walked, and in fairness to that turbulence I thought it best to know beforehand where I was walking to. For the first time I had the opportunity to hear spirit speak to me. "Simply walk into the hills," it said, 'see what you will see." And I almost laughed out loud as I realized that for the creatures of God, outside this poor and tortured world, the spirit is always conscious of your own awareness, and though perfectly discreet and by nature silent, it could always speak to you, sometimes subtly by a motion, as when you turn your head and wonder why you did, sometimes by a thought that obviously originated outside your mind, and just as normally but less in occasion, by voice.

I turned and made my way out of the pool. I was surprised to see little change in the world around me, for though I walked in both heaven and earth, I had, either unconsciously or by direction from spirit, decided to exert no control over this world for the time being. I was relieved that the steps I took were seemingly without influence on my surroundings. I appeared normal, although beneath my surface mind which now focused on the path ahead, I saw that my greater mind took notice of every atomic change the movement of my mind and body made, and kept a record of how those changes modified the universe. When I paused, my mind reported what it thought important about those changes and I chose my direction accordingly. In the near distance, I saw the hills where I would head. The path led south along the Jordan. I was walking without thought, spirit hurrying me on with a gentle force that made my motions effortless and swift. I noticed the sun set, and rise and set again. The journey seemed to neither have nor take much time, and soon I was climbing up into the solitudes of the Judean desert. I suppose it was wilderness, but to me it was like a low heaven, for the grandeur of its tumbled stone, and the mystery and fluidity of its sand. I saw the place I was to sit, a smooth hollowed alcove, worn into the stone cliff by wind and sand that had long since blown another way. I sat against the cool wall of stone; my back and body seemed to melt into it, until its reassuring strength described my position like a good chair. I was tired, and I closed my eyes to meet the darkness, still glittering with the sparkles of the desert sun, but fading after a while to a thick soft black, that, if I looked, I'm sure held the images of quiet stars.

When I awoke indeed the stars were out, bright and perfect. I was instantly awake, although I did not move. My mind raced across the events of the day, and I closed my eyes, this time in prayer. To think of God, now, was to see him, not in the sense of an exact image, but to feel in a seeing way the perfect nature of all things that are God. I know an ocean has often been used as an image of God, and I like the analogy in the sense that you can walk to the edge of the ocean, or you can wade in the ocean, or you can swim in the ocean, and each experience gives you the corresponding experience of it, and I like the concept that you might think twice about swimming into the center of the ocean with the intention of becoming one with it. But the fact is that the ocean is a three dimensional concept, even given spiritual qualities. But God exists, separately, both without and within. God is a vast universe of love. Outside that universe is anything unfinished. But the unfinished things are composed of bundles of energy that are wound from the fabric of the spirit. They may become part of God in an instant or in a billion years, at God's will. I was unfinished, so I was not God, but I now held what was this ruined creation's equivalent to God: Enlightenment. I could travel to the edges of God in an instant. I was one with God, although, being a man, separate from God. I was in union with him. Men have sought enlightenment and found it, what separates me from them is that I was born in perfection, and consequently when I came into contact with God, when I became enlightened through spirit, I stayed enlightened through spirit. No other man could maintain this, and the very impact of enlightenment on most men is enough to make them stop and think about it, thus reopening the rift of error. I did not need to make such an error. I had perfect spirit in conjunction with perfect body. I was architecturally identical to Adam, except I had no intention of ignoring a rule given to me from God's mouth. I had no intention of disobeying God in any way, and God had so far given me no rules, other than the law. If I did move toward doing something that would not harmonize with the will of God, then I knew I would be given warning. I knew this earth and its history, and no advice from anyone less than the Spirit of God, or God Himself, would be accepted without long and detailed debate. I had no need to make a mistake.

I stayed there for forty days, or so I am told, I myself took no count.

During these days I had time to realize how fully alive I was. I could wander the universe at will, at least in my finer bodies, but I saw no real need to do much of that. But I wanted to answer all the questions I had, about my childhood, about the reason I did not push harder for God in my young life, about why these extraordinary things were happening, and of course, what was I going to do now.

Most of these questions were answered when I did make one journey beyond the earth in search of who I really was.

The journey was short and I was at the beginning of time, no, more correctly, I was at the beginning of the beginning. I don't say this to be cute. Before time, which is a physical state, there was a beginning. In physical terms it was more than billions of years ago. Early in that beginning God made me. He woke me up to a reality where I was fully formed. I was a spirit, I suppose you could say. I moved with him, I watched what he did, I felt joy, and love. He passed the edges of things to come, and I would pause, fascinated, wanting to look deeper into these new things different. He urged me on with something like 'first this' as we continued to swoop around the universe that was He. After a while we stopped, and I existed as spiritual light, without thought or need to think.

Descriptions can be ineffective. It is better to actually be there, to experience, in order to understand. But for mankind being there will have to wait, for a short time, but a time that may overshadow many of you, so I give you what I can.

From light I was awoken again to the voice of God. 'Let us do now what you have seen'. So we revisited the places I had slowed to view, and I looked at what I thought I had seen, and as I looked they came to be, born along a few invisible lines that God had placed before my vision, like starting points, and as they came to be I felt my heart understand what God had wanted here, and with the help of spirit, which both carried out and suggested my thoughts, I began to mould the heavens. The heavens were the worlds around us. I gave them form, trying to give them the beauty and perfection of Presence that I felt God would enjoy.

And so we built the universe, and the beings I brought into being in my image began to help, and we toiled and lived for a long time, how long, I cannot say as I sit here. Ask your scientists, they will have a guess that gives the idea. But eons upon eons. And then we have the earth.

The earth was as far as we had gone. The earth was dense. We had taken the essence of the star, and bound these particles together until they had reached a density within which no movement had previously been possible. No movement, that is, other than the slow interplay between the elements themselves. This was one of the first worlds where we had created intelligent, separate movement of sentient creatures whose forms were composed of complex combinations of the heavier elements themselves. On other worlds we had creatures that skirted above or lived within or around the slow motions of metallic or gaseous environments. But their compositions had usually been quite simple, gas within gas or metal within metal, given energy from controlled chemical interaction, and consciousness. But on the earth the creatures themselves were composed of a wide range of matter, proportionate to the elements and compounds that made up the world itself, and were linked and confined by the same elemental laws that bound all dense matter. And out of this density we forced independent motion. We bound and rebound all the elements and combinations of the elements until we came upon motion. We compensated for gravity with complex use of bipolar energy linked to the mind and then further linked to spirit through magnetic force. We used water for strength and flexibility, and sunlight for transcendent energy. And spirit gave us the moulds, taken from the complex designs born of the heart of God. And we built, and we played, and we made living creatures, small and simple at first, but soon growing into complex forms, forms that we gave our own attributes, or fractions of our own attributes. The forms themselves soon began to take on the characteristics of living creatures, much like the worlds we had created before. But nothing as dense as the earth had ever grown so fine. What was amazing to us was that we became fond of, we loved, some of these creations and yet we lost them again to the energy of spirit, which brought about sorrow, and some doubt. In fact, we stopped before we made man. We who knew that man was the completion of this world. We looked at each other, hundreds of us, and looked to God. 'Go on', He said.

And so we finished. Adam and Eve. When the world was finished the release of concentration gave way to joy and celebration, we circled high into the highest of the worlds of light, and returned to look upon the earth. We were happy. It was good.

And then we all know what happened. The angel in charge of the earth's final visage, of its coverings as we called it, had fallen in love with the world and its beings.

He wanted it. He wanted to live in it and be its God. He wanted to feel the intensity of this world's love, and knowing how much we loved our God he knew how that would feel.

And before you know it, it was over. I spare you the details of the garden, for that you know, or will be shown in your final moments. When I saw what had happened I returned to God. I don't think I had ever been with Him in such an atmosphere of sorrow, though it was within me. 'What are we to do?' I asked. "It is done," He told me.

I returned to the earth and watched. How strong and sudden was the effect of action against the Will of God, and to our dismay, born on those who should have been innocent. We lost Able immediately, despite our warnings. Disarray is the wrong word, but I soon felt the hand of spirit, and I knew what I must do, and even as I knew I heard God say to me, "Go, and I will fix it." As I came closer I encountered who we now called Satan, and I could only reprove him to God, and I moved faster and faster until I lost all light, finally awakening, as I have already described, when I emerged from my mother's womb, blank, blank but for a glimmer.

My journey down to nothing had taken thousands of earthly years, and now, in the present, during this short journey to the beginning, I saw the history of the world without the gaps of my absence.

I was incredulous when I saw all that had transpired on the world since I left my position. I could not imagine the pain and torment that had been inflicted on men, innocent men, guilty only of being born imperfect, some struck down in that innocence, most maturing into little better than their captors, but all suffering pain that was never meant to be. Satan was enjoying his freedom and the exhilarating power of being able to, effectively, be thousands and then millions of people at once, cashing in their lives as one would eat a grape, oblivious, or more correctly, immune from the pain that each man experienced. The pain of the earth shrieked upward, as it does today, but we all have to wait until the day of God. I think what pained me most was the fact that so many men had learned to accept this debased and unnatural existence so completely, so easily. With such a little bit of favor, in the form of power and institution, Satan had bought off enough men to ensure that none, or very few, ever really doubted the finality and legitimacy of this dark and cruel reality. Men themselves would perform the task of keeping this world where it was. And what cruel irony that the agents of persecution and violence would act in the name of God. But God had kept aside a people, Israel, who had been told the certainty of Deliverance, that the day of God would come.

I was to ensure that The Day of God would come. Here I was, me again, and yet not me, but a body, a man.

I sat in the quiet of the desert, knowing who I was. In the dark night things crawled about me, malicious things, afraid to approach too close but enjoying the fact that they could harm me if I let them.

I was immersed in the world, in its good and evil. Its good was the residue of the original creation, its evil was the twisted things that had come to be, and the evil things that had made them what they were. I could transcend it all of course, but I had no inclination to do so, I was here to live as a part of this world and that is what I would do.

Near the end Satan came to me. He came as a quiet man, handsome even. He complimented me, saying that I had done well. I was physically tired and hungry, the world appeared more like a trance than what I remembered as reality, but as soon as I thought that thought, I noticed that all my faculties were intact, and I felt the presence of knowledge and spirit. Satan suggested that I should eat. I had the knowledge of all things physical, and could simply transform a stone to food, insinuating there was nothing wrong with that. And perhaps there isn't, I thought, but the next thought was, don't you think if God wanted you to eat, or you wanted to eat, that you could do better than a stone, not to mention that the scripture tells us man does not live by bread alone.

Satan grew angry with what I said, and I shuddered as a sudden force of noise and movement lifted me up from the ground, body and all, and we stood together on a battlement of the temple. "Cast yourself off," he urged. "No harm can come to you in your present state." I responded that the scripture warned against such tests of Our Creator, thinking how pointless such an act would be. Suddenly life shifted, and I felt a great happiness within me. We stood high upon a mountain looking down over a tranquil and serene earth. I felt the powers of love and strength pouring out of the lives of those below, and saw their castles and temples and great works, which emanated pride and achievement brought about by hard work and care. It was a good place, and I was enchanted for a moment. I could see not just what was in front of me, but it seemed I could see the whole world laid out, cities, townships, and humble cottages in numbers bewildering to the eye, accustomed as it was to seeing only what was between it and the quick horizon. "This is all mine," he said. "Is it not fine?" And without waiting for an answer, he added, "This is mine, acknowledge the greatness of what I have done as God of this world, and I will give it all to you, as to me."

I looked him in the eyes, and I will not say I felt pity, but perhaps I did, and I said with all my heart, "Satan, you know it is only God who can give us happiness."

# CHAPTER SEVEN

───────── ᏨᎡ ─────────

I was alone, my back once again against the reassuring stone of the alcove. I took a deep breath, and with it came the realization of how hungry and weak I was. I closed my eyes in prayer, and almost instantly I was able to tap into the vast reservoir of spiritual strength and power I now possessed. Joy sprang upon me, and with the uplifting of my spirit came the sound of music, sounds I had not heard in thousands of years, the sound of the angels in flight. After a time the sound became the tinkling of speech and I saw the bright forms hovering about me. Out of courtesy, the many became few, and took the more earthly form of winged maidens, radiant and beautiful, but with substance enough that I could see the variations of color in their kind eyes, and shades of complement in their long billowing hair.

I was fed the pure water that is incomparable to any food of the universe, and soft sweet bread to fill my body with strength and willing energy. It was a moment of purity and love, gratitude on my part of course, and a joy of such intensity that it struck the edges of the deep sorrow all spiritual creatures feel when they come close to the earth.

Within a short time I realized I had to get up. I was anxious to return to the world, to be about whatever I was to be about. I was already walking before I had given any thought to my destination. I kept going and was soon where I wanted to be, as is the way with things when harmony is present. I found myself looking down upon a valley of unimaginable beauty, stretching to a distant horizon that I knew was my direction.

In my life I had often seen the world with such clarity and spiritual enthusiasm that the light of the higher worlds shone down onto the images of what I saw. This diminished when I became more involved in the affairs of men, but returned on occasions when I had sought solitude and peace, or when events had gone well for the spirit and we rejoiced in a few moments of higher vision together. Now this vision was even more clear and tuned to the beauty of the earth. Since pictures of these images are not really descriptions of the natural world, or at least, they would be embellishments of them, I'm not going to keep describing what I saw as I traveled about, if for no other reason than the language makes it to difficult for me to do justice to what I saw, as I am no artist of the written word. I write only to deliver a message that I hope will clarify things for men in the last days.

But it was breathtaking. It was early morning and the sun was shining warm on my face, illuminating the rough valley ahead as I walked north and then east, back toward the river, and the place to which I now knew I was headed, the camp of John, where my new life had begun.

I took my time walking back to the little oasis where John taught and baptized. I enjoyed myself, and tried to think about what might be in the near future. Spirit had taken over my integration with the world, and though my being was still the operating center of the earth, it was no longer a conscious thing, and it seemed that in my normal movements of the day there was no noticeable effect on the world around me. I experimented with this a little, fascinated that the spirit could blend the massive spiritual force emanating from my being so seamlessly with my immediate environment that on the surface I seemed like any other man. But the new spiritual center of the earth was having its effect on earthly reality. Al things were moving according to their decisions based on the new information given them by their own spiritual awareness, although this awareness was for them, on the most part, unconscious. Even I did not see this great alignment taking place, for I had not thought to look closely at it in my meditation. I knew that what had to be would be, and this would be monitored and guided by the spirit and by God. I also knew it would be well, and that if I needed to pay special attention to anything I would be given a nudge or even spoken to by spirit to make sure I considered what must be considered.

But I was interested in the way I had sunk so invisibly into the ordinary. I remembered my first few actions when the spirit had entered me at the baptism pond, and all the cataclysmic and visual effects these motions caused, and I remained amazed to see this had virtually disappeared. My experimentation showed that I could still summon up the immediacy of pure spiritual and physical power. The motion of my staff through the air could quickly attract force that became intense if thought was focused on the action for a purpose. I drew clouds from the far reaches of the desert and sent them scuttling on past my view. I formed them overhead, so that they swirled around the vortex that the motion of my staff created. I even ignited the little storm I had created with a forceful thought that brought a clap of thunder and a sharp flash of brilliant light to the tip of my staff. After that, I had a moment's fear that I might have overstepped my purpose, and I dropped the stick and moved to a nearby rock to think. After only a few minutes of contemplation and a return to the serenity of the consciousness of God, I had a first long look at what I was about to do.

I knew that my people expected me, for I had studied with them in the temple and talked to them in their homes. It should be a joyous time I thought, and I didn't look much further into the future, as I felt more interested in living the experience than examining it from above. I was excited. But there was something more to it and as I searched for what I sensed, I travelled higher and higher into the worlds of heaven, until I was near the throne of God. Now I did not see God, but from a place of great beauty that was once again the world, I heard my father say, "It is I who have sent you here, and what I ask of you is to do my will. You are my son and you will not do other than my will, for I know you." At first this was a little cryptic, even for me, but as the words spread back to my earthly mind I realized with clarity that God was explaining exactly what I had been thinking about earlier, trying to determine my boundaries, testing my thoughts and actions to see my limitations, or lack of limitations. God had made it clear to me that I was to do nothing other than respond to events passively, and that those reactions would be in accordance with his will, which would manifest itself in my natural responses guided by spirit, but I was to take no active role in correcting or disciplining this world. I saw that God's purpose for me was to allow the true nature of this world to reflect itself upon me. I was to let the world react to me, and again, what would be, would be. Although I had the power to reshape this world in my image, for the time being this was not what I was to do. I was to be obedient to God.

Speaking about God was something I wanted to do, so I got up and continued toward the oasis, but I did not hurry. My power and strength had not diminished, in fact I felt a certain freedom with my new understanding of God's will, and I played for a few days or perhaps weeks, with the desert and the sky, with the breeze and the scent of the desert flowers. In view of my new understanding of my role I needed no instrument to concentrate my energy or attention, or to lean upon for strength. It was a wonderful time and even though the season was late, I felt no cold, and suffered no hunger. I was like a bird playing in the whirlpools of the sky enjoying the embrace of the wind, and happy to see my food prepared when I grew tired.

But I was ready when I spied the camp ahead, and again I felt excitement as I thought about seeing men for the first time since my baptism. I walked around the camp, through to the nearest village, where I rented a clean, modest house for a few small coins. The house had a pleasant main room, furnished with a strong table and several chairs. For the first time in months I bought my own food and provisions, and went to bed on a fine soft mat.

I awoke to a cool bright day. I washed in leisure, enjoying the luxury, and retired to the front room to meditate and pray. Around noon I made my way to John's camp. This time I took the path that wound through the low hills, dotted with a few trees, still green or green tinged with orange as was the nature of the land at this time of year. As I approached the area where the pool began, a small stone wall edged the side of the path to my right, where the hill remained ascending and the path had been cut level to afford entrance to the area around the lagoon. As I was drawing close I saw John look up, and speak to the little group of men he was with. Although I was out of ear shot for normal hearing spirit brought the words to me with clarity, "Look, the Lamb of God, who takes away the sin of the world! This is the one I meant when I said, 'A man who comes after me has surpassed me because he was before me.'" [5] The words filled me with appreciation. He indeed knew who I was, and, leaving out things of little import, was telling these men that I had a prehuman existence. Although I do not think they understood, this showed me again his directness and honesty.

I spoke to no one that day, and retired early to my new little home. The next morning I came again, and John was again there to notice my coming. This morning he was talking to two men only, and my eyes immediately fell on them. They were striking, not simply for their physical appearance, but for the way they displayed a visible harmony with body, mind, and spirit. Again John struck to the point as only the true seeker can, "See, the lamb of God." [6]

As I continued on my way the two men broke off from John and hurried after me. Seeing them follow me I turned to them and asked what they were looking for. 'Where are you staying?' [7] they inquired. 'Come and you shall see,' [8] I answered.

And so it began. John had given me everything to make it easy for me to approach the nation as a teacher, and now he gave me a gift in men, the first of my disciples, Andrew and John.

When we reached my house we reclined on the divans the house supplied. I brought the thin wine I had purchased and offered them some of the quite good bread I had also bought. We were all happy and excited, though I did not show it, and conversation went quickly and brightly as it does when you find yourself with those with whom you have a lot to share.

Our talk did not take long to get to the point, but I will take a moment.

This seeker, a disciple of John, and also called John, was an imposing figure. He was fair for our people, with short curly hair and bright light eyes not common to Jews. I was impressed with him, I think because my recent past had been so lofty in a way, and so concentrated on the failings and futility of man, that I was a bit surprised, and joyful, to see that a man could remain so pure and accurate in his thinking and perception as far into his life as John obviously had. He spoke of nothing but The Way. Each word was spoken in order to bring back into the present moment the urgency and importance of finding Truth and God. He spoke to teach, until you caught up, and then he would question you with open happiness to find our how deeply you shared his knowledge and vision. But his speech was never heavy or ponderous; each word was filled with light and a deep joy, as if he knew that what was being spoken would bring happiness. He knew the scriptures so well that they were woven into every thought, indiscernible from normal reason and logic but lending a power and authority to his words that made it hard not to believe what he was saying and want to learn more.

Andrew was very different, small in stature and quick with action, word, and eye. Like John, he was very handsome, and had a confidence that made it easy for him to be the first to act, and easy to accept that his action had been the right one. Only Peter, his brother, was more quick to thought and action, and more sure of his feelings. And that is the way it would be with all my disciples, the twelve, I mean. They were gifts to me from God. They helped and supported me, and talked for me. They relentlessly pushed me for the truth, knowing, I suppose, that in time they would learn the Truth from me, and thus from God, their goal. When I referred earlier to my creative power going out into the world and invisibly realigning things to take into consideration my spiritual dominance of the planet, the disciples were as good a practical example of this as you can find. Now when spirit aligns things on such a scale, time is not a factor. These men were chosen and prepared for me before they were born, although it was not manifest and brought into action, in terms of present time, until just a few months before. There was much they did not know, of course, and the kind of things I needed to teach them do not come from an afternoon seminar. They must be learned with the turning of the world. They must be taught by a mind and spirit that knows what is to come upon the wheel of life and positions itself between the student and the moment, to catch the meaning and illuminate it forever in the mind and soul of the student. This I could do.

Soon, satisfied with my answers, John asked me, 'Who are you?' 'The son of man,' I replied. A silence followed. They thanked me and left, Andrew not trying to contain his enthusiasm, and John, leaving his happiness for a more careful meditation, but awed, and beginning to see the magnitude of what he thought might be true. It was dark when they left, but it could only have been an hour before I heard voices at my door. There was Andrew, leading a man by the hand and saying, 'This is he, Simon, this is the Messiah.' I looked at the man who was being led so unceremoniously into my house. Simon was about the same height as John and also thin and fine looking. His hair was longer, and his lean face was shaped by an almost sharp intensity and was it not for the kindness of his eyes I would have taken him for a warrior. He smiled and a great blast of light came with his white teeth and bright deep eyes. He stood and looked at me for a long time, and then his eyes dropped to the floor, displaying the great gentleness that lay beneath the energy of his personality. I almost had to laugh at the affection I felt for him, so pure and strong was the intelligence and warmth I saw behind the power of his aura. This was a man who believed he was to be one with a great power, a universal power, and nothing smaller than the universe was going to stop him, but I could see that he knew, somehow, that that universe was love. The power of my own being stopped him for the moment, though, and I could see that he accepted me at that very instant, although his mind would have to understand that acceptance before he could be happy. "You shall be called Peter," [9] I said, because he was like a piece of the rock that is God.

There was nothing left to say that evening, but I told them I would see them in the morning.

I saw that John the baptizer and I were not to come together, and I did not question spirit about it, because I knew that it had to be. I did not want to bother him any more, for my presence kept him from work he had to do, and I did not want to make him sad in any way. That night after the men had left I saw in prayer that I should gather up my few things and proceed to Galilee. I was also told that along with Andrew, John and Peter, three other men would accompany me. With that thought in mind I cleaned the house and prepared to depart in the morning.

By the time I got to the camp in the morning a small group of men were seated around a large fig tree not far from and just above the water. I noticed Peter there and when he saw me he began to approach, and all but one man, who was in meditation under the tree, followed him toward me. I headed for a comfortable spot where we could sit and talk, and reclined on one of the rough wooden benches assembled together for just such meetings. Soon the group approached and I met them, one by one. They were an impressive group. Even as I speak about it I become joyful in remembrance. These were beautiful men, each one individually the type of man that one would remember and likely even comment on, but together they had such an effect, not just visually but on all the higher senses, that I couldn't stop a smile from spreading across my face as I looked at them.

His brother Andrew and two other men accompanied Peter. The first was introduced as James the brother of John. James was unlike his brother, except perhaps for the quiet power they both possessed. James was tall and slim and dark. His visage seemed to be carved from ebony, and he appeared to loom a little, not so much from his height, but from the deep blackness of his eyes, which shone with intellect from beneath the angled brow and helmet of black thick hair, eyes that you had to look at, and from which there was no escape, so still and thoughtful and silent were they. He was as quiet as his eyes, but when he did speak, everyone around him was silent for a moment while they considered the magnitude of what he said.

The other man was Philip. Only slightly taller than James, but heavier in girth. He had short cropped hair and a short beard, and, I think much in the same way as I just described my feelings, he was a bit overwhelmed with it all, translating the strong emotions he felt into a thin smile that was likely to erupt in great chuckles of laughter whenever something seemingly outrageous was said. And many such things were said. The mere mention of the messiah, or the coming of the kingdom of God, not to mention following me as the son of man, were enough to bring a great fit of laughter from Philip. His head would rock up and down as his body rippled with happiness and amazement, and some justified uncertainty that would soon be verbalized with his great deep voice. "You mean to tell me that God is bringing about the purification of the whole priesthood?" he would boom in amazement, looking to the side as if to get his bearings and then turning his head back to meet his partner in conversation with great gleeful eyes. When Philip was not so engaged he was slow and thoughtful, quiet, and content to simply go about his business. He volunteered little, but watched, and acted with strength and loyalty when needed.

The four of us talked for several hours, Philip brought food and wine around midday, and soon it was decided. They would go with me to Galilee, the decision being made simple for them by the fact that they all came from that area. This made it easier to come with me without confessing that they were fascinated and drawn to every word I said, and by my person, and that the true hope, almost too good to be true, was welling up inside their hearts, that I was indeed the Teacher.

We adjourned to prepare for our journey, and I noticed Peter and James go to the man I had seen under the tree, who was now standing beside the water talking to a group of Judeans. I watched as Peter spoke to the man, who looked toward me, obviously doubtful about what they were telling him. As they approached me I said, 'Here is a true Israelite, in whom there is nothing false.'[10] I said it so that they heard me, and as they grew close the man, Nathaniel, asked me, 'How is it that you come to know me?'[11] I told him that I had seen him under the tree, and I went on to tell him a little of what spirit had shown me he was considering in his meditation. The accuracy of what I told him concerning his own thoughts astounded the man, and, so certain was he of his own well earned powers of discernment, that he instantly said, 'Teacher, you are the son of God, the King of Israel.' [12]

This was Nathaniel, tall and powerful. Not heavy, but his body was of the nature of Taurus, so strong that his head was bent slightly forward from the pull of the muscles in his neck and torso. There was not a hint of humor in Nathaniel. He was serious and certain. The wickedness of the world was plain to him, and for some years he had put away all triviality, and focused his entire mind and strength on discovering, and overcoming, whatever had caused this world to be so without apparent purpose or justice.

In reply to his heartfelt faith in me, I responded, to the whole small group, 'I tell you all truthfully, you will see the heaven opened up and the angels of God ascending and descending to the son of man.' [13] This was enough for them, and we left that very day for Galilee.

After crossing the Jordan we headed north, for Galilee. The weather was clear and beautiful, the worst of the cold season seemingly over. The path was easy for the most part, and we took our time, enjoying the adventure of the journey and the fellowship that was growing between us. I paid attention to everything around us, to the trees and the sand, and the small red desert flowers that bloomed along the path, to the wind and the sun, and the colors of the day that shifted in golds and yellows and mauves against the hills. As I paid attention to these things I made them a part of me; I extended my light out into the world with full consciousness, not enough to distort or change the natural world, but enough to make it alive and under my will. I brought a brilliance and newness to our environment that could not help but be noticed by the men. I was aware of every movement of every leaf and every cloud, of every animal that stopped and peered at us as we passed, and every smell that the perfumed plants gave to the cool breezes to waft across our path. I made each moment a moment of awareness and awe, so that my companions always had something to notice and discuss. I showed them with the power of spirit the greatness of the universe, and the majesty of this all but unspoiled corner of the creation. We were lifted, not above the physical world, but into a deeper core of the physical world by the power of my will. I did all this with the full consent of God and spirit, and it also taught me more about God's designs for my behavior on the earth. Of course my friends were delighted, the spiritual nature of the energy around them leading them to conversations and reasonings on the nature of our world, and on our lives, and on the deeper things of God. It was very good. I felt no constraints upon my power, and I relaxed to an intuitive certainty that my will and the will of my father were now in accord, and that I could do and say and act and exert power as I pleased, without fear that I would be in conflict with the limitations given to me.

This journey set a model for much of my remaining life. Other than the joy of giving the truth to interested men and women and seeing them understand and accept it, these were the happiest of times for both me and my disciples, enjoying the fellowship and love and learning, as we moved beneath the vast open sky of God.

As we entered into the territory of Galilee, I was told, not without a fair amount of excitement, that in talking to a group of families travelling in our direction, Peter and Nathaniel had discovered that a wedding was taking place in Cana, Nathaniel's home town, and that, indeed, my family was to be there. Due, I suppose, to the considerable interest being generated in the vicinity about this man Jesus, and not outside the normal standards of hospitality among Jews, Peter also told me with great enthusiasm and some concern that I would accept, that we had been invited.

It was a large wedding, with family and friends coming from some distance to bring their blessings and their joy to the bride and groom. For the Jews, weddings were the happiest of times, and there was great merriment around the house.

The feast itself was held outside, in a large walled courtyard with high white stone arches leading into a covered area where people reclined and talked and sang. The arches were laden with a white climbing flower just in bloom; no doubt the wedding date was set for the early blooming of this scented flower. Bright torches lit the walls, and light poured from the interior of the great stone house. Everyone was in their finery, and being the cool time of year with the clear dark sky cheering the gathering on with its bright array of stars, that meant long tunics and bright sashes, covered by thick fine robes of every color.

Of course I was pleased to see my mother again, and my four brothers, although beyond an embrace and several assurances that all was well with me, we discussed my life only a little. I think even my mother was a little hesitant to dampen the occasion with talk that could lead to concern or sombre matters. My friends were enjoying themselves, rather cautiously though, wanting at once to tell everyone present about the stirring ideas they had been sharing and anxious to talk about me and the events at the camp of John the baptizer, but polite, and hesitant to steal the attention away from the celebration.

I know that most of you know what happened next, so I want to take this moment to make another footnote. What I did and said for the remainder of my human life is well documented in the scriptures, whose verity is not in dispute. If you have not read and understood the sacred scripture, I suggest that you make a point of doing so, in order that anything you read and understand here may have benefit to you. You may have to search for those who truly know the Bible, and can explain it, for they are few, and yet many if you keep an open mind. Since my words and deeds are so well recorded, I am not going to repeat these things, unless I feel it is necessary for the context of my story or worth repeating for some reason, be it for further explanation, as it will be in some cases where I am not well understood, or if spirit directs me to include some text or other for deeper reasons of its own.

My disciples—I call them that now for after the miracle of the wine whatever few doubts remained among these six were erased, as far as the human mind can be free of doubt—were overjoyed and filled with new pride and certainty because of my display of power. As I mentioned before, I too, was learning the boundaries of what God expected from me, and although there was no doubt that what occurred was designed to occur, I had concerns about the triviality of the miracle itself. These made me conscious of the fact that, the symbolism of the power to turn water to wine being established, it was unlikely to happen again.

The next day was a day of rest for all. My mother and I met in the afternoon and had a meal together, during which she asked me all the questions she had wanted to ask me the day before. I assured her I was well, and explained to her that my slightly cool response to her at the wedding sprung not from lack of love or devotion, but from the Truth. She took my fairly long recollection of what had happened since I left our home in stride, although she did break into tears, be it from joy or sorrow or precognition I do not know, perhaps all three. Almost inaudibly she spoke. "This is what has to be, Jesus, and I will pray for you every day, never doubt that, but please, son, be careful, you are my life itself." It was an emotional moment for me as well, worldly feelings tearing at the heart as they gave way to greater ones. Our conversation quickly changed to brighter things, and with a voice suddenly filled with more playful notes, she told me that she and my brothers would like to accompany us on the journey to Capernaum, where they were going, in any event, to spend some time with yet another cousin.

After another restful day and the reorganizing of our provisions, our somewhat larger group set out on the road to Capernaum.

Capernaum By the Lake, as some called it, was a beautiful place. Its white, well built houses moved up from the Sea of Galilee to the hills and the plain above, and further followed the roads that led off toward the world. It was an active place, with a fairly large Roman outpost and a tax office. Many of the houses were modeled on Roman architecture, which I admit lent a certain beauty to this already beautiful spot. At the same time that it was a city, Capernaum afforded a certain isolation, for, as the town spread down to the sea its inhabitants were virtually all Galileans, as they had been for centuries, and Galileans maintained their identity and their privacy. I knew Andrew and Peter lived in Capernaum, making their living as fishermen. James and John also lived nearby, just to the south, at a spot where the Sea of Galilee lies gently at the foot of a long fertile plain. The sea is so clear and placid at this spot it was often called the Lake of Gennesarat, after the lush green plain that rose above it.

When we arrived at Capernaum I sent the men to visit their parents, while I went about locating a place for me to stay, for I had known even as we approached this place that Capernaum would be the center of my efforts to reach the people of Israel. I was lead by spirit and my own inclination to a small white stone house, not unlike the one I had occupied near the camp of John. It was to be my home, if home I had. I paid the owner of the house enough to secure it for what was to be the rest of my life. For me it was a good place, deserving the name Capernaum held as one of its meanings, 'the village of comforting.' My brothers spent some time with me, helping to make the house comfortable and suitable for an itinerant life, but capable of holding quite a few people in relative comfort.

After the festivities at Cana, I wanted to re-establish a more appropriate mood for what lay ahead. It was not long before Andrew and Peter found my home, and the next day the six friends and I took our midday meal together. After we had finished, I brought them together in silent prayer. Prompted by spirit, I concentrated in prayer with the desire to bring us together in purpose. Almost immediately the spiritual intensity of the moment increased, bringing bright light into the room, and with the light came a series of questions that could be heard only as the silent voice of spirit. The voice was not my own, but I recognized it as Pure, and allowed It to continue with the aid of my own mind and spirit, knowing the instruction that was to come was what I had requested, and Sacred. The questions were not unfamiliar to any of the men, but they were certainly not used to the way in which they were being addressed, by a force entirely internal, powerful and clear, and yet without any physical signs of sound or source other than the light that suffused the air around them. The questioning went on for some time; a thin synopsis would sound like…. 'What is it you are looking for?' then 'What is God's purpose for this world?', and 'How will his kingdom be restored to the world?' The answers came from the collective wisdom of their minds, prompted by spirit if confusion or shyness kept the words from coming up within them; and they went something like this…. 'We are looking for the truth of God, to live perfectly in the perfect world of the loving creator,' then, 'God's purpose is that the earth be restored to its original state, perfect and eternal,' and, 'His kingdom will come when he exerts his will upon the earth on his Great Day of Judgement,' and finally, 'His Rule shall be brought to the earth through the Son of Man, the Messiah.' I encouraged the peace of truth to fill the room, feeling humble and a little surprised by the power of the event. The questioning stopped, being replaced for a time by a tangible feeling of warmth, and love. Such a thing never occurred again in my lifetime, but it forged a bond between us that lasted and remains.

Before we set out to Jerusalem to attend the approaching Passover, as was required of adult male Jews, and which law I would certainly observe as his Son, I needed these men to fully realize the importance and significance of my going there, and to have faith in the truth of what I said and did. It is a difficult thing for a man or woman to accept that the Will of God has manifested itself in a human who appears just like themselves. Even if the fact is accepted in the day, when the light is clear, such a thing still has to be remembered and accepted all over again when one wakes up the next morning.

I knew my purpose was to tell the Nation of Israel that God had responded to their prayers and their prophecies by allowing a representative of His Own Will to come to the earth. This One had the power to forgive the imperfection that causes death, and the power to lead imperfect man through a transformation of the existing reality into the True Reality, a Reality without death, without pain, and without end. I needed my disciples to truly understand this, and know I was this Person. The small miracle spirit performed in bringing us together that first meeting in Capernaum gave me faith in them as much as they in me, and a part of me relaxed as I turned toward the future.

# CHAPTER EIGHT

A week later we once again took to the road, only this time our destination was Jerusalem. It was hard for me to believe that I had not returned to the temple since I was twelve years old. God had his reasons, I knew, and at the time I was not inclined to search further for them, the present fully occupying my attention. The mood was good. All along the path were the families of Israel, bright with enthusiasm over their own journeys. And of course it was spring again. My disciples were happy and excited, almost like children wondering 'What will he do? What will he say?' To be honest, I had no firm intentions, other than to observe the Passover. Naturally I knew I would do as I must, and I was equally excited at the prospect of seeing the temple, and of course I would teach.

As we walked into the outer courtyard, in awe, as virtually anyone would be, I had to stop. Instead of the sacredness increasing as we looked toward the inner temple, there was clatter, and makeshift stalls, and the jumbled whine of haggling. Sheep and cattle were everywhere, and the moneychangers sat before huge bowls of coins, as if the purpose of the temple was to deal in profit. I knew it was required for each worshipper to offer a sacrifice to the alter, and that for the poor and for many of the travellers hurriedly flooding into Jerusalem for Passover it was sometimes difficult to find an offering or a money changer, but I also knew the temples of God had existed for centuries without the defilement I saw before me.

I felt no hesitation from spirit, and taking a multi-thonged rope from a man who was evidently a seller of cattle, I methodically knocked over the first few stalls, and began to drive the sheep and cattle from the temple courtyard. "Will you make my father's house a house of merchandise?"[14] I asked the sellers. Richly dressed men approached and asked, "What sign do you show us, since you are doing these things?"[15] "Break down this temple, and in three days I will rebuild it." [16] I replied calmly.

It was a hard thing for me to do, for I knew I made no friends that hour, at least among the Pharisees who made a great profit from the selling. But it was a symbol of what was to come, and it was required of me.

I did not know what was expected of me, or what I should do. My disciples and I continued with the preparations for the Passover meal, which began the next day at sunset. I had sent Andrew and Peter to find a room where we could celebrate the Passover, and use as lodgings for the next few days. They returned late in the afternoon, and by the time it was beginning to get dark, the seven of us headed down a series of winding stone streets toward our rooms. Since it was the evening before the feast, all Jerusalem was alit. Every house was bright, with light pouring out the windows of the thick stone walls that lined the streets and towered above us. Beautifully clad men and women were hurrying about, just as we were, making sure everything was ready for tomorrow. As on all Passovers, the moon would be full, and so tonight the great yellow orb hung above the city, as merry as the worshippers below. In all the history of man there has never been anything as great as the people of Israel coming together for a festival before their God.

At dusk the next day the Passover began with the evening meal. I reclined with my six friends before a great table, set with velvet and adorned with silver goblets. Two great silver candle holders sat near the ends of the table, and large silver wine decanters held the sweet red wine that would be passed between us, as was the recent tradition. I could not but notice that the introduction of red wine to the ceremony, which was not required or even mentioned by Moses, must have been a silent prophecy, in order that the Jews become acquainted with the wine that was to represent the blood of their Saviour. My attention to this detail turned out to be intuition, for wine was used on my last Passover as a symbol of my blood, and then as an obligation forever. But I was not thinking of such things at the moment. I was enjoying the wonderful banquet my disciples had prepared. It was so beautiful in every detail that I was surprised. These men were more enterprising than I had given them credit for. When the sun had set and everyone was clean, we informally positioned ourselves around the table and began our meal. Of the rituals, I will mention only one, the scriptural command: "And when your children ask you, `What does this ceremony mean to you?' then tell them, `It is the Passover sacrifice to Jehovah, who passed over the houses of the Israelites in Egypt and spared our homes when he struck down the Egyptians.'"[17]

It had been a difficult week. I was still upset over the incident at the temple, for the next day I had had a visitor, a Pharisee who stayed long and examined me with well-considered questions. He had expressed faith in me, but as I reviewed our conversation I began to think more deeply into what actually lay ahead, and I was disturbed. Soon my disciples could see that I was troubled and finally one of them simply asked, "Master, what is wrong?" I looked long into his eyes and finally laughed, the evening was so wonderful, was it I who would spoil it? We ate and drank and talked and sang, as is the way. Later in the evening, when we were quiet and content, John asked me, "Really, Master, what is it?" I looked at him again, and began to tell him.

I knew from my study of the scripture, before my enlightenment, that the son of man would not be well received. He would be crushed, and carry the sickness of the world, and I knew now, from the vision of spirit, that I must be sacrificed for the purpose of giving the world a new start. But what I really hadn't expected was that Israel might not recognize me, and by Israel I mean their priesthood, which had always been the heart and soul of the nation, the ordained intermediary between the people and God. Would they actually not accept that I was the Messiah? I knew from experience who I was, and so I had unconsciously thought that, since it was true, God's representatives on earth would ultimately accept my status as the Son of God. But as of late I had begun to be fully aware of what had always been there in the back of my mind, that it may well be that Israel would never fulfill its own prophecies. I didn't tell all to John, but I did explain that we needed to spend time in Judea, to further the knowledge of those living around Jerusalem concerning my coming. We all talked about our future plans, the men pleased that they were being included in the decision-making. By midnight we were in agreement that we would remain in Judea after the Passover and make a concerted effort to reach the Judeans with the message that the Messiah had arrived. The six were determined that we should baptize people in the fashion of John, as they were used to, and I agreed, although I myself would not baptize, for my baptism was to be of a different nature.

The next day we proceeded to the temple late in the morning. I was pleased to see that no sheep or cattle were being sold in the courtyard. My disciple, Andrew, in fact, had heard on the street that many had long objected to this new and unscriptural practice but had done nothing about it until now, and they had taken this opportunity not to allow the livestock back into the temple, at least until further discussion.

We made our way through the Court of Women and into the Court of Israel where I had sat and talked many years before. I found a spot and began to pray, and my disciples did likewise. After they had finished their prayer, my disciples rose in unison, as we had arranged the night before, and set out to talk to these men of Israel. The basic approach we had agreed upon was that the men should ask all those who would listen, first about John the baptizer, then about the One whom John had prophesied would come behind him. Did they know that John had now declared that that One had arrived? Did they know that that One was the Son of God and the Redeemer of Israel? Had they heard of Jesus? Did they know that I was in the temple? During all this I was to remain stationary.

At a prearranged moment we all came together and walked from the inner court out into the courtyard. A considerable group of men followed us. The disciples approached those outside with the same discourse they had used within. After a while, as we had also decided the night before, John raised himself up to speak. John was a fine orator, well versed in the scriptures and the law, and he spoke with a brightness and intelligence that was contagious. Within a few minutes hundreds of people were listening. Finally he looked toward me and said, "This is He, the Son of Man." At that point I began to teach the listeners. What I said you have heard before and will again, but it was not so much what I said but how I said it. As I spoke I opened my vision to the full brightness of spirit in silent prayer. Soon there was a glow of light around me, and around the disciples, who were standing near. The brightness grew until the temple building itself, just behind and above, began to glow with the pale clear light associated with the presence of God. When I had finished speaking the entire courtyard was silent in front of the illuminated temple. Without a word we walked together out the temple gate, where our belongings had been brought for us. We continued through the busy streets and out into the countryside of Judea. In scripture this event is only spoken of as, "viewing his signs that he was performing."[18]

Our hearts were light but introspective as we came into the green countryside and the warm afternoon sun. We traveled later than usual that night, and in the morning we walked until we came to a small body of water, beside which we made our camp. The following day, after a relaxed morning of food, prayer, and fellowship, the disciples made their way to the surrounding towns and roadways, approaching everyone they saw, and speaking to all who would listen. These men had been the disciples of John the Baptist, and they were trained in bringing the attention of the local population to their teacher. With their new enthusiasm and knowledge of the events dawning over the land, they were now even more effective. Within a few days there was a substantial crowd around our campsite, and I gave John and Peter permission to baptize as many as they could. After as many people as we thought were likely to come were baptized, and advised of the coming of the Son of God, we traveled on until we came to another likely spot with the availability of water suitable for baptism. We did this for nearly eight months.

On the Sabbath of the 240th day after we left Jerusalem, I received news that John the Baptist had been imprisoned by Herod. Three days later we began our return to Galilee.

It was a long trip home, the weather fickle and sometimes cold, not unlike many of the people we had encountered. But we were a very satisfied group. Not only were we very close to each other, we also felt that we had done a difficult job, well. One thing we were confident of was that Judea knew about us.

After a few days on the road we were deep into Samaria, which is a barren dry place in many areas, and we were tired. Since we had arrived near the town of Sychar, known to be the site of the Well of Jacob, we sought out the well, and, sending the disciples into the town to buy food, I decided to remain and spend time in prayer and meditation beside the well that had been dug by the very father of all Israel many centuries before. I had not been there long when I noticed a woman approaching. As she lowered her bucket into the well I spoke to her, "Give me a drink." She was surprised, but bold, and said to me, "How is it you, being a Jew, ask me for a drink when I am a Samaritan woman?" [19] I looked at her and I liked her. She was obviously intelligent, and pretty, despite the signs of a difficult life. I was prompted to speech.

"If you had known," I answered, "who it is that says to you, 'Give me a drink,' you would have asked him, and he would have given you living water." [20]

"Sir," she replied, "you have not even a bucket for drawing water, and the well is deep. From what source, therefore, do you have this living water? You are not greater than our forefather Jacob, who gave us the well and who himself together with his sons and his cattle drank out of it, are you?" [21]

"Everyone drinking from this water will get thirsty again," I pointed out. "Whoever drinks from the water that I will give him will never get thirsty at all, but the water that I will give him will become in him a fountain of water bubbling up to impart everlasting life." [22]

"Sir, give me this water, so that I may neither thirst nor keep coming over to this place to draw water," she responded.

I now said to her: "Go, call your husband and come to this place."

"I do not have a husband," [23] she answered.

I knew that what she said was true, and spirit instructed me to look at her deeply, and I saw much. "You said well, 'A husband I do not have.' For you have had five husbands, and the man you now have is not your husband." [24]

"Sir, I perceive you are a prophet," [25] the woman said in amazement.

Revealing her spiritual interest, she noted that the Samaritans "worshiped in this mountain which stands nearby, but you people say that in Jerusalem is the place where persons ought to worship."[26]

"The hour is coming," I said, "When the true worshipers will worship the Father with spirit and truth, for, indeed, the Father is looking for suchlike ones to worship him. God is a Spirit, and those worshiping him must worship with spirit and truth." [27]

She seemed genuinely impressed. "I know that the Messiah is coming, who is called Christ," she said. "Whenever that one arrives, he will declare all things to us openly."

"I who am speaking to you am he," [28] I told her, as directly as I had spoken to anyone before.

When she noticed that my disciples were returning, she turned and went her way back to the town. I smiled, and when my friends arrived I spoke to them, pointing to the town and the fields around it. I asked them to note that the fields were ripe for harvest, and that already the reapers were in the field, collecting wages. I did not simply mean the barley in the field, for it was a time before it would be ripe, but I spoke of the white color of the grain, and more, for what I saw, and perhaps some of them saw, as they looked where I pointed, was the white color made by the spirit working over the town, going to the minds of those who were receptive and making them aware of me. It was a welcome sign, and for John and Peter who saw as well, that our work had not been in vain, and that a great harvest was being prepared, and even though the grain was not ripe in terms of the calendar, indeed it was nearing the time, and our harvest would be one of men. The sign was a source of rejuvenation, made even stronger when within the hour many of the men from the town came to us and asked us to remain with them for a few days. At the end of our stay the men of the village openly confessed that I was the savior of the world, and many of them truly believed.

When we reached Galilee a few days later I sent the men to their homes. I stayed in the hills and thought and prayed, rebuilding my strength and sharpening my focus on what needed to be done.

When I was full of spirit I turned toward Cana, where I stayed until the man spirit had told me to expect arrived. The man was an official of the King, Herod Antipas, and he lived in Capernaum. He had heard that I had returned from Judea into Galilee, and he had rushed to me for help, for his son was very sick. When I saw him I barely listened to him before saying, 'Return to your home, for your son is healed.'[29] On the way home he got word that his son had recovered, at the very hour I had spoken to him. The next day I left for my own village of Nazareth.

Foresight is a thing we all know a little about, and I don't want to elaborate on that too much here, but I can tell you that I was a little nervous about going back to Nazareth. I suspect the feeling of unease had as much to do with what I had already come to learn about men, especially religious men who feel they have a special status bestowed by God, than from any hints given me by spirit. But I tried to be positive. I showed up at the synagogue on the Sabbath as I had every Sabbath before my departure to the Jordan River. The congregation was excited; it was obvious that word had reached Nazareth that I had come home. We all greeted each other in a friendly manner, and when the service began I was asked by the overseer to read, as I had often been asked to do, especially after my father Joseph died. I was handed the scroll of the prophet Isaiah, and here the spirit came into play as I noticed the illumination of a passage I knew well. And so I read,

The Spirit of the Sovereign LORD is on me,
because the LORD has anointed me

to preach good news to the poor.
He has sent me to bind up the brokenhearted,
to proclaim freedom for the captives
and release from darkness for the prisoners,
to proclaim the year of the LORD's favor
and the day of vengeance of our God,
to comfort all who mourn,
and provide for those who grieve in Zion--
to bestow on them a crown of beauty
instead of ashes,
the oil of gladness
instead of mourning,
and a garment of praise
instead of a spirit of despair.
They will be called oaks of righteousness,
a planting of the LORD
for the display of his splendor.
They will rebuild the ancient ruins
and restore the places long devastated;
they will renew the ruined cities
that have been devastated for generations. Isaiah 61:1-4

Then I stopped reading and spoke. I explained that to Israel was to come One who was anointed by, or chosen by God to restore Israel not only to the glory it had had while David and Solomon ruled, but also to a glory of which that rulership was but a symbol. The house of David was to establish true justice on the earth in God's name, not simply for a few generations, but for all time, and that the 'desolation' referred to in the scripture meant not simply Israel's defeat at the hand's of an earthly army, but the fallen state common to mankind that has brought death upon us all. And then I said, "Today is the fulfillment of this scripture." [30]

It seemed to please the congregation, but within minutes of the end of the service, I felt the machinations begin. 'This is the son of Joseph, is it not,' [31] was said with no feeling of affection but as an expression of doubt that I should, or could, aspire to such heights. And if I was truly such a man would I not have preformed great deeds and said great things when I was among them? Most of the talk came from men who valued their position in the congregation and were used to accepting all the praise that came their way. It was not seemly to them that I should claim to spiritual greatness without coming to them for permission, or to bestow thanks on them, or even better, to perform miracles as payment for all their priceless spiritual guidance. They never considered that the things they taught me they were obliged to teach, just as someone had taught them without need for reward. It took only a portion of an hour for all these things to be thought out and become 'the position' of many of the older men. When I pointed out, scripturally, that during the drought Elijah was sent not to a widow of the women of Israel but to a native of Sidon, such was the mystery of God's will, they became angry. I was astounded at their reaction. I had had anxiety about coming home, but I never expected this, for they rushed upon me and took me outside to a high cliff where they tried to throw me off. I was never in any danger for I knew spirit had no intention of letting them kill me, but I had to exert myself and dull their senses in order to avoid just that. It proved to me, though, just how tight a hold Satan had on men of authority, and how they had no real power of reason if he called upon them with true intent, for I knew he was about.

After my escape I again took some solitude, relieved, in a way that my visit home was over, and a little surprised that my intuition had been correct but had underestimated the violence of what happened. But now I felt free. I could think of no further ties to the earth that needed to be unravelled, and I felt comfort in the fact that my disciples were men I could rely on to help and rely on to learn. And so the next morning I turned back toward what was now my earthly home, Capernaum. I was ready to begin my work in earnest, just as someone who has tried out the full circuit of a track returns to the beginning to see how well it can be run with full effort.

I soon found Andrew, Peter, John, and James at their boats in Capernaum. I was feeling strong and enthusiastic, and I wanted no hesitation from these men to match my zeal, so, as you probably know, I urged spirit to give the men enough fish to keep John's father, who owned the business, happy for a long time, although I knew he was a righteous man who would expect or require no such gift. As I had already set up the house in Capernaum, I asked them to join me, and we began preaching immediately. I had filled them with light as well as the fishing nets with fish, but this was hardly necessary because now it is I who would take the lead in letting the nation know that the Kingdom of Heaven had indeed drawn near.

The next Sabbath we attended the large synagogue in Capernaum. I did not hesitate to begin teaching the congregation, and I left no room for the kind of criticism I encountered at Nazareth. But opposition came from a different quarter. On this Sabbath a demonized man was present. After a while, he shouted with a loud voice: "What do you want with us, Jesus of Nazareth? Have you come to destroy us? I know who you are--the Holy One of God!" [32] The demon controlling the man was actually one of Satan's angels. Rebuking the demon I said, "Be quiet, come out of him!" [33] The demon threw the man into a convulsion and yelled at the top of its voice, but it came out of the man without hurting him. Even my disciples saw a new authority to my teaching.

After the service Peter rushed to me, obviously distressed. His mother-in-law was gravely ill. We all proceeded to Peter's house, where I saw that she was indeed sick. I took her hand, and spirit healed her instantly. She got up enthusiastically, and felt so refreshed she wanted to show me her appreciation by preparing us all an evening meal. By the time we had eaten it was dark, and while the lamps were being lighted we saw a large crowd outside. To our surprise, there were hundreds surrounding the house, for word had travelled quickly about the healing of the possessed man, and the whole town was aroused. I went outside with the four and began to heal the sick. I do not know how many were cured of their disease, but it was many. Some of the people were possessed of demons, and I ordered them out. As they left they called out, "You are the son of God," [34] but I did not let them speak further, for they knew me, and it is up to each man to come to believe on his own accord, neither was it appropriate for them to herald the arrival of the son of man.

It was late when I arrived home, but I could not sleep, due to the force of spirit generated by all that had occurred. I got up before dawn and walked down to the beach, to an isolated place, to pray to my Father. Before the sun rose Peter and the others found me, and Peter came to me to tell me that all the people of the town were looking for me, because they wanted me to stay with them. I had the disciples sit with me for a while, and I explained that I must go to the other towns and cities around us, for it was not to enjoy the company of a friendly village that I had come to earth, but to teach as many as I could. They understood, and assured me that they wanted to join me wherever I wished to go. When we returned to Capernaum the people besought us to stay, but my disciples helped to explain why we must go, and soon the crowd dispersed in a good mood.

For the next few months we taught across Galilee, and many came to believe. The spirit healed, without partiality, the sick and infirm wherever we went. Soon it was not possible for me to stay in a town or city, because the throngs would become too much. Instead I found the high and lonely places and slept there, usually allowing my disciples to stay with friends in town, although Peter and John often chose to remain with me. In the mornings I went into the towns to talk and heal, and usually I would withdraw before dusk. On occasion we would take a meal at someone's home, as guests, Andrew and Peter being adept at deciding who was trustworthy so that we could relax for a short time in the comfort of a house without causing too much of a disturbance. People were searching us out from all parts of the country, from Judea and across the Jordan, from Perea and Decapolis, even from as far away as Syria. On occasion we slipped away and took a boat back to Capernaum, once again Peter and Andrew showing initiative by obtaining the use of a sturdy boat, and of course all four were experienced sailors. When we did arrive at Capernaum it was usually not long before our presence was discovered and crowds would quickly assemble to listen or to be healed, or simply just to watch.

On one occasion I had gone to the beach and spent the morning talking to the crowds that had followed me out of Capernaum. As I was on my way back to town, I passed by the tax office. The tax collector was sitting in a small booth outside the building, the weather becoming warm again, and he looked at me as I was passing by. I could see that he knew who I was, and his large black eyes became soft as he looked at me. Through spirit we exchanged thoughts, and without hesitation I walked to where he was sitting and said to him, "Be my follower."[35] Equally without hesitation he stood up and entered the building behind him. A minute later he came outside and stood in front of me. "I have turned in my position as a tax collector", he said, "I will follow you."

Matthew was a large man. Although he was not tall, his body was massive and powerful, his thick neck a seamless continuation of his jaw and head as it joined a chest and stomach as round as the girth of two men. He was as strong as any man I had met, and yet his eyes were those of a great calf, gentle and almost melancholy. And that is how he was. Strong of body but gentle and mild of heart, with a deep understanding of scripture that came from unusual effort and stamina at study, and most importantly he knew God, and placed this knowledge above all else.

We continued on together to the house, where I left him on his own to meet the disciples. That very night, Andrew informed me, we were to dine at Matthew's house.

It was a lavish gathering. Matthew had invited as many friends as would come and the majority of the men were tax collectors or other officials, for the people in general disliked such men, or any man that dealt with Rome and as a rule would not associate with them. It was a wonderful meal, with luxuries we were not used to, nor inclined to, but it gave us an opportunity to discuss the truth with men and women it was difficult to be close to under normal circumstances. At the end of the meal, all of us aglow with the pleasures of food and drink, I thanked Matthew for the reception, and smilingly but seriously said to him, 'There will be few such meals as this from tomorrow on, Matthew, is that well with you?' He looked down for a moment and then said to me, his great brown eyes moist with sincerity, 'This world is only dust for me if I cannot please the living God; I will follow where you go.' And from that day forth Matthew was with us until the end.

Time had passed and the Passover was again approaching, so we began making preparations to leave for Jerusalem. As we were doing this three disciples of John the Baptizer came to us. After they had eaten and felt rested they asked me, 'Why is it that we and the Pharisees practice fasting, but your disciples do not fast?'[36] In answer I said to them, "How can the guests of the bridegroom mourn while he is with them? The time will come when the bridegroom will be taken from them; then they will fast."[37]

I saw that the question, like most, had many levels. On one level they knew that many of John's disciples had come to follow me, and it was natural for them to be upset by that, for it would make them wonder if what they believed was true, so they wanted to see if they could find flaws in my teaching. Also, they were worried about John, as he had been imprisoned for some months now, and they were trying to see if we knew what might become of him. Added to that, they wondered why we would not at least fast while John was imprisoned. Did we not care?

My answer was fair, as it was John himself who had referred to me as the bridegroom, so they would understand the reference. But by my answer I also wanted to allude to my death; that they might think about this later, and believe.

I went on to say, "No one sews a patch of unshrunk cloth on an old garment, for the patch will pull away from the garment, making the tear worse. Neither do men pour new wine into old wineskins. If they do, the skins will burst, the wine will run out and the wineskins will be ruined. No, they pour new wine into new wineskins, and both are preserved." [38]

I said this for two reasons. First, I wanted to explain that my teaching was fundamentally new, and its conclusion would be the fulfillment and thus, cessation of the written law, the cornerstone of Judaism. The teachings coming out of my ministry would not be a patched up form of Judaism, but an entirely new level of awareness of God. Also, I wanted this saying available in scripture, for it would explain to men in the future that, in the last days, the world must realize that no institutions, or structures of thought, or codes of conduct, or even physical understanding of the nature of life itself, would be carried into the new world. The New World will be just that, a new beginning for man, as if he had just been born into a newborn world.

A few days later we left for Jerusalem. We left well before the Passover so that we could stop in the towns of Judea and preach in the synagogues along the way. Things went well, but as we came to Jerusalem an event occurred that became the theme for my undoing. There is a pool near the 'sheep gate' of the city that was believed to have healing properties. It was the Sabbath when we passed by this pool, which was called Bethzatha, and I was called to a man who had been sick for a long time. He was so weak that he was unable to lower himself into the pool at the appropriate time, as the others would push him out of the way whenever he tried to go in. I cured this man and instructed him to take up his cot and leave the place. As he was leaving, the Pharisees reprimand the man for carrying his cot on the Sabbath. Later, when he learned that it was I who had healed him, he went to the Pharisees and told them it was Jesus who instructed him to carry his bed.

On the day after the Passover meal we were at the temple, and a large group of Pharisees approached me. When they had determined that it was I who healed the man by the pool, they began to reproach me. Now I thought that perhaps they would inquire as to how I cured the man and come to see that it was through the spirit of God that I did these things, but, no, they became even more hostile. Since we were at the temple I did not want this base and unfounded anger to go unanswered, and I gave them a thorough response. As I said earlier in my story, I am not going to talk about every scripture that is written about me, but this one sums up many things, and illustrates well the obstacle I encountered with the priests of Israel that eventually became insurmountable. I may make comments during the scripture but the record of this account covers the things I wanted to say. I am making a special point of this interchange because these were the things that I had been so troubled about on the previous Passover, and that I had spoken to John about, namely that I was beginning to have real concern that the Judeans would perhaps never accept me, and in my response to this new assault I wanted to make a real attempt to show them how important it was that they understand I was not a threat to them, but indeed, was a part of their own faith.

In my response to the Pharisees' accusations that I had healed on the Sabbath and ordered the man to carry his cot, the record is this:

*I said to them, "My Father is always at his work to this very day, and I, too, am working." For this reason the Jews tried all the harder to kill me; not only was I breaking the Sabbath, but I was even calling God my own Father, making myself equal with God. To this I answered them "I tell you the truth, the Son can do nothing by himself; he can do only what he sees his Father doing, because whatever the Father does the Son also does." John 5:17-19*

Now I said this because I had been aware, since shortly after I came out of the wilderness, that although I had the power to do things issuing from my own will, God had commanded me, while I was on the earth to do things only as I was directed by spirit, which would reflect the will of God.

*"For just as the Father raises the dead and gives them life, even so the Son gives life to whom he is pleased to give it. Moreover, the Father judges no one, but has entrusted all judgment to the Son, that all may honor the Son just as they honor the Father. He who does not honor the Son does not honor the Father, who sent him. "I tell you the truth, whoever hears my word and believes him who sent me has eternal life and will not be condemned; he has crossed over from death to life." John 5:21-24*

While on the earth, despite the fact that I would only do things as directed by spirit, which were the will of God, the people who listened to me and believed, I could accept, and through that acceptance they would be offered the water of life, which was mine to give as I had told the woman at the well.

*I tell you the truth, a time is coming and has now come when the dead will hear the voice of the Son of God and those who hear will live. For as the Father has life in himself, so he has granted the Son to have life in himself. And he has given him authority to judge because he is the Son of Man. "Do not be amazed at this, for a time is coming when all who are in their graves will hear his voice and come out--those who have done good will rise to live, and those who have done evil will rise to be condemned. By myself I can do nothing; I judge only as I hear, and my judgment is just, for I seek not to please myself but him who sent me. John 5:25-30*

Here I talk about the fact that I will have a life and a will after my earthly course is complete, and that it is then, when the new world is ushered in, that I will judge those who will have life and those who will not, but even then my will is the will of my father. I wanted this out in the open, for the Sadducees were not really acquainted with what I taught, and they did not believe in the resurrection, so I thought it better for them to know this now than for it to be a thorn later.

*"If I testify about myself, my testimony is not valid. There is another who testifies in my favor, and I know that his testimony about me is valid. "You have sent to John and he has testified to the truth. Not that I accept human testimony; but I mention it that you may be saved. John was a lamp that burned and gave light, and you chose for a time to enjoy his light." John 5:31-35*

As you know, I had great affection for John the Baptizer and appreciated the fact that he accepted me as what I was, with a full witness. The Pharisees had recognized John to some extent, and he had told them about me, and yet they would not listen to him about this.

*"I have witness weightier than that of John. For the very work that the Father has given me to finish, and which I am doing, testifies that the Father has sent me. And the Father who sent me has*

*himself testified concerning me. You have never heard his voice nor seen his form, nor does his word dwell in you, for you do not believe the one he sent." John 5:36-38*

I went on to remind them that even above the testimony of John they should be able to recognize me by the great things the spirit was doing through me. They could not accomplish the things I could, and yet they would not believe.

*"You diligently study the Scriptures because you think that by them you possess eternal life. These are the Scriptures that testify about me, yet you refuse to come to me to have life. I do not accept praise from men, but I know you. I know that you do not have the love of God in your hearts. I have come in my Father's name, and you do not accept me; but if someone else comes in his own name, you will accept him. How can you believe if you accept praise from another, yet make no effort to obtain the praise that comes from the only God? But do not think I will accuse you before the Father. Your accuser is Moses, on whom your hopes are set. If you believed Moses, you would believe me, for he wrote about me. But since you do not believe what he wrote, how are you going to believe what I say?" John 5:39-47*

I express my frustration with them, for they claim to be the teachers of the word of God and, indeed, they are learned in the Holy Scriptures, but they seem to pay no attention to them. If a Pharisee they did not know visited them from another town, they would give him respect and listen carefully to what he said. And yet they will not even consider what I say, despite the fact that, scripturally, they know a Messiah is soon to come from God, one worthy of great glory and respect. Finally, I warn them that if they truly claim to believe the Bible, it is the very words of Moses that will condemn them.

All that I say to them only increases their opposition, and they become firm in their intention to kill me. Within a few days we left once again for Galilee.

Being the time of Passover, it was full springtime in Judea, and we were happy to be under the great blue sky, observing the rush of growth in the countryside. But our joy was short lived. As we were walking, the disciples had grown hungry, and in the spirit of the moment they had picked a few heads of grain, and after rubbing them in their hands to remove the chaff, they nibbled on them as we walked. It was not long before an angry group of Pharisees approached us. 'Look, your disciples are doing what is unlawful on the Sabbath,'[39] they cried out. I answered them, but I will not go into detail, I think you get the idea.

And so controversy over the Sabbath, the sacred day given to men as a time to appreciate all that God has provided for them, a time for joy and fair thought, continued to grow as the excuse for my persecution. I suppose in fairness it should be pointed out that it was on the Sabbath we had the majority of our contact with the religious rulers, for we always attended the synagogues on that day, but none the less, the irony is strong.

It was on another Sabbath that we attended a large synagogue near the Sea of Galilee, having made our way up from Jerusalem and now approaching our home. In the congregation there was a man with a withered right hand. Watching closely, the Pharisees finally could contain themselves no longer, and they asked me, 'Is it lawful to cure on the Sabbath?'[40] Now they were comparing the miracles that I had preformed through spirit to the normal practice of medicine, which people by tradition did not do on the Sabbath unless it was life threatening, the tradition having being taken to the extreme that a sprain or a broken bone may not be bound or set on the Sabbath. The man looked at me, and I asked him to stand up before the congregation.

"If any of you has a sheep and it falls into a pit on the Sabbath, will you not take hold of it and lift it out?"[41] I asked them. There was an answer, correctly given, that the scriptures say a good man is caring for the life of his animals, so I continued. "How much more valuable is a man than a sheep! Therefore it is lawful to do good on the Sabbath."[42] No one answered, and I said to the man, "Stretch out your hand."[43] He stretched it out and the hand was healed. Now there was in attendance that day a Sadducee, one of the elite group of Jews most closely associated with the priesthood, who was also a member of the Court of King Herod. Immediately after the services he went to the political body of the Court of Herod and there they conspired to kill me.

The next day Peter brought me word that the Sadducees and the Pharisees were united against me, and that they had joined with officials of the state to kill me, for every man in Galilee knew about me, and it was not possible for them to keep such a secret. Upon hearing this we left for Capernaum, although we did not go directly to my home, for we did not want them to find us while they were still full of enthusiasm for my death.

After a time we returned to teaching, and great crowds came from all the country around to hear me speak. Many of the people believed, and the four had been teaching those who were sincere, so there was a band of followers who remained in Capernaum constantly, being in the hundreds. Nathaniel and Philip had joined us, and they helped with the organization and education of the many who considered themselves my followers. Most of them had some sense of my message and purpose, and of who I was, and of those most had knowledge of the scripture, and of the living God who had created the earth and chosen us as his people. Those who did not have knowledge of the written law were being trained by the six, or by someone well versed in the Truth who had been assigned to teach, either by myself or one of the six. All were instructed in meditation and prayer, and the reasoning that went with the knowledge that the Kingdom of the Heavens had drawn near.

Soon the crowds had grown so large that I asked Andrew to find boats for our use, so that I could teach at the lakeshore, a few yards out into the water. This prevented the people from crushing ahead trying to get closer to me, and also, it was good near the water's edge, the sky and sand and water creating a natural theatre where I could easily be heard, for the weather was fine. With the boats we moved from spot to spot up and down the coast and reached many, and were able to satisfy the need to hear for all those who sought to listen. My four great fishermen did indeed become fishers of men, and even I did not know, the months before when I had said this to Peter, that it would have such a literal fulfillment. I simply could not have reached so many people in such a pleasant and successful way had it not been for the great skill with which the men handled the boats, Peter often standing behind me overseeing the gentle rowing and paddling that was required to keep the proper distance and position from the shore. Both he and John were always there, standing tirelessly, their handsome faces shining with spirit and appreciation, not only for my powerful words, which came directly from the spirit of God, but also for the men and women who listened, watching the faces of the crowd and seeing the dawn of hope and happiness that came over those the spirit touched, and remembering to seek them out later to help continue their movement toward the Way.

It had been about a year and a half since my baptism, and I came upon a time of reflection. I withdrew into a mountain that was close to Capernaum, a place we often sought out to relax and talk because of its great beauty and comfortable glades. I walked to the top, where I sat under the stars of heaven and prayed and thought until the dawn.

With the increased hostility of the Pharisees, and their new alignment with the State of Rome, I began to see, and spirit did not deny it, that I did not have too much time remaining. I considered what had occurred and what lay ahead. I saw that my life had fallen into two portions. One was the teaching of the people, and the other was reaching out to the ordained Ministers of God that were His Priesthood. In Israel priests officially represented God to the people. They did not take this upon themselves, but were given this responsibility by God. After coming out of Egypt, it was the Living God who gave the sons of Aaron, from the tribe of Levi, the sacred duty of acting as God's agents to the people of Israel. Even as I walked the earth there was not a priest of Israel that was not a son of the sons of Aaron. My Father had ordained these priests, and I could not put them aside. So while I was pleased with the success my ministry was having with the people of Israel, I would not be legitimately accepted by the nation unless the priesthood accepted me. And it was these very men, or the agents of these men, who had designed to kill me.

I knew what the priests wanted. They wanted me to give a great sign that would signify that I was restoring God's Kingdom, and that being the case, they could look forward to becoming the Priests to a nation that would for all time rule the world with the Power of God. But this I could not do, for it was not God's will that this old wineskin be patched up to receive the new wine of eternal life. But neither was it God's will that they reject me. In God's name John had called out to them, 'Repent for the kingdom of heaven is near.'[44] The priests were quite entitled to hear the words of John and repent, for God had by no means taken that choice from them either by will or prophecy. But I saw that Satan had taken hold of these men just as he had the priests of the great temple of Solomon before it was destroyed.

So despite my pleasure at the fact that the masses were listening to me and being uplifted, that joy was badly marred by my knowledge that whatever gains I made with the people would be undone if the priests succeeded in triumphing over me. For make no mistake, the crowds that came to me were not free, as they appeared to be, they were on a leash, and the leash was made of chain and blood and when the leash was tightened it could not be resisted without great power. As went the priests, so went the nation.

But I could abandon neither path. I would most certainly teach the people, and I would impart to them the glory of the good news, that it was they who would inherit the earth, though at present they were oppressed and downtrodden. For those who desired good, their suffering would lead to eternal happiness. And I would not give up the Nation; I would reason with the men of power until I had no breath.

As I was thinking these thoughts the sun covered the green land before me with all the colors of the glory of the dawn, and I rose up and went down the mountain with the intention to organize what I had, so that all things might be accomplished.

When I reached Capernaum I called to me the closest of my followers, and there were about seventy. Of them I chose twelve to be the inner circle of my disciples, whom I had chosen in prayer the night before, and they became known as apostles.

I chose Peter and Andrew and James and John and Philip and Nathaniel and Matthew, whom you know. And I chose Thaddeus and Judas and Simon, and Thomas and James.

Thaddeus was a great man, and in another time he would have been a king. He was handsome, as the world judges beauty, as were they all, except perhaps James the smaller and Matthew and Judas. He had great power and stillness and spoke no word without reason. When he did speak it was as the warm breeze that comes off the ocean with the late sunlight. Thaddeus knew that when the mind and spirit are united it brings things into being. He was the warmest of them all.

Judas was a powerful man, with an eye for anything that was truly fine. When he was happy he was generous, and he loved music and the things that made song. When he found a musical instrument that was made by inspired hands, he knew it, and would treasure it and keep it safe. He was tireless at work, and careful that all things were done as they should be. Of the twelve he was the only one that was not a Galilean, being a Judean.

Simon was a man of force and fire, with a mind that knew what was true and what was false no matter how subtle the covering. He was a warrior, but his knowledge of God had made him sweet and gentle. He was tall and fair, and no eye that fell upon him could resist him.

Thomas was small and slender. He was careful and thorough, and had mastered the art of making things, especially from leather or coarse linen. He learned carefully and thoroughly until he knew about a thing, and then he was its master. Thomas enjoyed the conversation at the day's end, and could find the error in any argument if it was there. Women loved Thomas for they knew he would be the best of husbands, but he did not marry until my life was over.

And there was James, called the lesser for his small size, though it applied in no other way. James was the happiest of the twelve, and the gleam from his light eyes was rarely missing. He had fear of nothing, and enjoyed the challenge of the riddle, as did no man. James seemed to dance or skip when he walked, and whenever I spoke with him I could not help but smile, and with the smile there always rose the bubble of joy that was his gift to impart to others. He also loved music and could play beautifully, although it was not often we could enjoy this because our lives were preoccupied with the work at hand.

When I had chosen the twelve we went to the foot of the mountain where I had spent the night in prayer, and a very large crowd followed us, many of them from a great distance. When the twelve had settled around me, and all the people around them, I closed my eyes to draw spirit to its full attention. I instructed them, and the people around them listened. I spoke both to incite them not to be discouraged by the things of this earth that appeared to be true but were not, and to teach them lasting principles. What I said was later to be called the Sermon on the Mount, although it had no significance beyond what was said.

With the help of the twelve I was well organized to deal with the large crowds of people that came to us in Capernaum, for these twelve also instructed the other disciples to teach and make the word firm and productive in any man that sought to learn.

Some weeks later the disciples and I were traveling to the towns around Capernaum when we came to a town called Nain. As we entered the town we encountered a funeral procession, and I learned that the young man who had died was the only son of a woman who had recently lost her husband as well. She was in agony of despair, for not only had she lost those she loved most, but with the loss of her son she would face a future of uncertainty and poverty. I was moved by her grief, for she was a good woman, and these things were brought upon her only by the random acts of the unkind earth. I approached her and as she looked up at me I saw a spark of hope reignite within her, and I told her to stop weeping. As I approached the boy I felt the strength of spirit grow within me and the joy rose within my own heart at what I knew was to occur. I said to the boy, "Young man I say to you, get up."[45] And he sat up, and his body was fully restored to a clear state, and he began to speak as one who wakes up but does not know where he is. Word of this miracle spread quickly throughout the whole land, because raising the dead was something beyond anything they had heard of me, and it was worthy to the people of great chatter. News of this deed reached John the Baptizer, who was still confined to prison, and he sent two of his disciples to me inquiring, "Are you the one who was to come, or should we expect someone else?" [46] When I heard this I asked that my disciples spread out and bring me all the sick and infirm people they could find within the area, and when they were brought to me I healed them all, the blind and the deaf and the infirm. I then told John's disciples to return to him and report what they had seen. All the good of mankind are waiting for deliverance, and John, who was the best of men, was also in hope that I, as the son of God that he knew I was, would be able to exert a spiritual power that would be able to dispense instant and permanent invulnerability to those on the earth who were pushing toward, and worthy of, this deliverance. But really it was not until after my death that the true and sacred secret of the scriptures came to be revealed. God is the God of True Justice, and this must always be true for it is not possible for God to ever be unjust. The Justice of the Universe had been served upon the earth as it must be, perfectly, and that perfection illuminated that the conscious choice of Adam to disobey God's clear and reasonable rule, that he have dominion over the earth and all things within it, but that he not eat of only one specific fruit, was an error. The condition of the earth was exactly, nothing more or nothing less, than the simple consequences of that action. That does not mean that God, and every spiritual creature in the universe are not devastated by the pain and suffering, and the meaninglessness of the reality resulting from that error, they are. But what is of more importance is that no such thing occur again, for all eternity. When Satan convinced Eve to eat of the tree, to the aware it was clear that what he was saying was that this rule, this one and only rule, was not made for the good of the creation, but for some reason that served God's own interest. He said that, in fact, God was lying. For God warned man that if he ate of this tree he would die, but Satan said, "You will not surely die."[47] When man ate of the tree he did die. God did not kill him, his action did. But worse than that, Satan stated that the rule did not serve the best interest of the creation, and that God knew it. "For God knows that when you eat of it your eyes will be opened, and you will be like God, knowing good and evil."[48] Satan made it appear God did not want this; despite the fact man would like to be like God. We know the first part was true, that Adam died, but would eating from the tree make man like God? Many today insist that this is true, that men are Gods and Goddesses. The only way to determine if God's motive in making the 'rule' was truly for man's benefit, was to see how things turned out after it was broken. If men would ultimately become Gods, there might be some argument that 'the rule was not in man's best interest.' For, it could be said, despite all the pain it took to get here, look, 'we are Gods.' Satan still works to convince people that they are, or will be, God. God has allowed the choices of man and Satan to be left alone to work out their own destiny. But the truth is, this destiny will be utter degradation and suffering, for the planet and for man. It has nothing to do with God. People on the earth are fools to think that death and suffering are part of some secret design of God. I have already spoken of these things, but they bear repetition.

Ultimate degradation for the planet and death and suffering for man (Satan does not die as man does) were not conclusions satisfactory to God. But God could not intervene without breaking his own laws of perfect cause and effect, and more importantly, because God may forgive the effects of the laws of cause and effect if he wishes, but if he did, if He intervened, Satan could, and would, say that God simply did not give him enough time to work out his plans, and that if God had stayed out of it, he would have brought the world to a place that was actually superior to what it was in the beginning, and man to Godhead. And thus nothing would be settled. And so it is today. Make no mistake, there is no physical deliverance for this earth until the entire universe can plainly see that, regardless of what Satan says, both man and the planet are doomed. When it is evident the planet is beyond saving, and all men are doomed, God will be vindicated and the words of Satan will be shown to have been lies, entirely untrue. If the 'rule' had not been broken, man would have been nurtured to a perfect future, well precedented in the worlds of God that have existed for time upon time. And once the rule has been shown to be valid, and of good intention, and the premise that God may make a rule for its creation proven as Reasonable and Just, then, in no other creation, physical or spiritual, throughout eternity, will God have to allow such allegations as were made by Satan concerning the earth to stand. He will be entitled to simply step in and say, "No, so and so creature, I have made this one rule for your benefit and you must obey it. Because my integrity cannot be challenged in making this rule, look at the record concerning earth. Satisfying your will in this case does not justify all the suffering that will come about because of your mistake," and God may proceed to forgive this creature's mistake, if he does break the rule anyway, or not, as He sees fit.

When the precedent of our world is established, God will be justified to step in, anywhere in the universe, at any time, and, if someone is reasoning that some rule is not a 'fair' or 'good' one, God may explain that a rule made by the Creator is fully within His rights, and He does not have to allow it to be broken. We need never go through such a nightmare as the earth again.

So where did this leave the earth and mankind? Exactly where we are. Except that, His nature being Love, this was not acceptable to God. And so He arranged that, without interfering with the so called evolution of this world, He would still save it. And that is where I came in. I came to the earth and was perfect. I had no error built in from the genetic necessities of my physical body and I broke no spiritual law. Yet I was brought to death. This was an action of Satan's world that was equal to the mistake made by Adam. Thus God was able to resurrect me, as a man, from the dead. And as a resurrected man I am a part of this world now and for all time, and when the moment comes when the entire universe shouts, 'No more, the world is doomed,' I will come to this world and save it, for I am a man and I have the right to do this. I will stop its slide into nothingness, and I will rebuild it atom upon atom until every justice has been done and every wrong made right.

But until then I could not simply release John from prison and give him the solace and reward he deserved. What I said above is the sacred secret that is contained in the scriptures, but John could not know that, for, as I have said, it was not known until after my death, except in generalities. So I grieved for John and sent him word through his disciples that the blind were being made to see and the lame were being made to walk, and that the scriptures were being fulfilled.

While we were still in Nain, I received an invitation to an evening meal from a certain Pharisee named Simon. I was pleased to go, for the occasion would afford me the opportunity to discuss the things of God with not only Simon, but with the many others who would attend the banquet, for he had a large and luxurious home. When I arrived I saw that my assumption had been correct. The main room was filled with men and women, many of them Pharisees, and my position at the table had been arranged so that many of the men reclining at the tables would have the opportunity to hear what I said, and to speak to me.

As I entered, however, the tone of the evening was set by the fact that I was not able to wash my feet, which was our custom, seeing that the roads are hot and dusty, and I had travelled some distance to his house. This would be even more appropriate at such an elaborate dinner, where the furnishings and woven materials were fastidiously clean and obviously valuable, and where the host had servants, as was the case here. But I was not concerned with this and took my place, enjoying the pleasant surroundings and looking forward to perhaps breaking down some of the hostility the men felt for me. During the course of the meal, a woman approached my divan and kneeled down at my feet. I looked at her as she began to touch my feet, and I saw that she was a woman who had sinned often in the manner of having relations with men who were not her husband, and had shown no remorse for her actions. As I looked at her she began to cry, and I had pity for her, for I could see that she was a good woman and had a sorrow about her, in that despite her boldness, she was afraid that she was ruining her life, but did not know how to change things. As I thought this she began to cry with greater intensity and her tears fell on my feet. Taking her long hair in her hands, she cried for some time and wiped the tears from my feet with her hair, drying them. After this she took oil from an alabaster jar and proceeded to rub the oil onto my feet. To the people of my day the rubbing of oil on the feet of others was a common expression of courtesy, or affection, so the incident did not shock anyone in the room, but I saw from my host's eyes that he was thinking that if I were a true prophet I would know what kind of woman was touching me, and reprimand her as a sinner. So I said to him, "Simon, I have something to say to you." [49]

"Teacher, say it!" he responded. "Two men owed money to a certain moneylender," I began, "one owed him five hundred denarii, and the other fifty. Neither of them had the money to pay him back, so he canceled the debts of both. Now which of them will love him more?" "I suppose," said Simon, with an air of indifference at the seeming irrelevance of the question, "it is the one to whom he freely forgave the more."

"You judged correctly," [50] I said. And then turning to the woman, I said to Simon, "Do you see this woman? I came into your house. You did not give me any water for my feet, but she wet my feet

132

with her tears and wiped them with her hair. You did not give me a kiss, but this woman, from the time I entered, has not stopped kissing my feet. You did not put oil on my head, but she has poured perfume on my feet. Therefore, I tell you, her many sins have been forgiven--for she loved much. But he who has been forgiven little loves little." [51] I again turned to the woman and said, 'Your sins are forgiven.' [52] The men at the table began to mumble that who was I to forgive sins, but I said to her again, 'Your faith has saved you; go your way in peace.' [53] After this the meal proceeded, but little was accomplished to further their understanding.

As I was returning to the place where we were staying I saw the woman waiting for me, and I sent my disciple, John, who had accompanied me, to bring her to me. As she approached she was again in tears, so I asked her name, to which she answered, Mary. Now I further inquired where she was from, and she told me she was from Bethany, near Jerusalem, and that she had a brother and sister there, named Lazarus and Martha, but that she had left the place because they had grown angry with her because of her sinning. I told her to return to her home, and tell them all that had happened, and that they would accept her.

After these things I began to go throughout Galilee as if in a great circuit. I took with me my twelve and there were others that traveled with us, to help and to learn. Many of them were people I had cured, and they were grateful and had faith in what I was doing and in Who I was. There were also women that went along with us, and they provided for us with their own possessions, and they were a source of strength to us. We travelled from village to village, and I cured many, so that the controversy about us became great, and many scribes and Pharisees came to us from Jerusalem, although, it became apparent, simply to discredit us. Even my brothers came out to find me, because they had heard about all the things that were going on, but they wanted to lay hold of me, and force me to return to Nazareth, because they were of the opinion that I had lost my mind. But because I was healing those with incurable disease it was difficult for even the Pharisees to deny the power of the spirit, but they began to say that I was casting out demons in the name of Beelzebub. Despite my pointing out the impossibility of this being the case, they persisted in saying such things, and I observed that spirit itself had a great anger for these men because of the things they were saying, and that although I could come to forgive them, they had become condemned, for spirit would not forgive them, because they spoke against the spirit.

I continued teaching and the people received me well because they were being cured, and because their lives were tiresome and my words gave them hope. But I was concerned; for I knew that when I was gone it would be difficult for them to remember with faith, for they were not getting the meaning of my words. So I began to teach them with illustrations, hoping that by speaking in this fashion they might remember my words and continue to think about the things I told them, as a man might do with a riddle. I first gave them the illustration of the seed that is cast, pointing out how some of it would grow and some of it not. This illustration was based specifically on the results I had seen with the many we had taught: although they heard the word, for one reason or another many would not produce the fruit of the teaching. I knew that at the center of this resistance was the fact that without the religion of the land embracing my words, the heart of the people had absorbed almost all that it could sustain. We did not give up, however, but continued to teach with increased resolve, for if even one heard and understood, and came to know and believe the truth, the reward was worth the effort.

I had been teaching now for some two years and I wanted to reach as many as I could before the obstacles I saw in my path prevented me from giving further knowledge to the people. So I divided the twelve into twos, and sent them out to wherever they could go within Israel to talk in the synagogues and on the roadways and at the doors of the households of the land. I sent spirit with them, and told them not to prepare with either gold or sword, for the things they needed would be provided. If they preached in an area and were not well received, I instructed them to continue on, leaving nothing of their hope behind and without looking back. But in many areas they were well received, for people were curious because of all the wonderful things they had heard, and I had given the disciples the power to drive out demons and to cure the sick. Their faith was strong and they were able to do these things.

It was slightly before our third Passover together and I was awaiting the return of my disciples so that we could prepare for our journey to Jerusalem, when I heard that John the Baptizer had been beheaded. I was deeply grieved when his disciples brought me the news, and for three days I retired to solitude, not to set a model for any behaviour, but because I wished to be alone with my God and my sorrow.

Very soon the twelve returned to Capernaum, and they were full of enthusiasm when they saw me, for they all had stories to tell, and wanted me to know all the wonderful things they had accomplished. Well as soon as they had arrived at the house the crowds began to gather, and although the disciples were tired and hungry I knew we would not be able to even have a meal together in peace, and so I told them to prepare the boat and we headed off for a place where we could be alone and they could have the pleasure of comparing their journeys and experiences, as they deserved.

When we landed a crowd had already gathered, for some had seen us leave and run along the shore and others had followed. As we made our way up the hillside the crowd grew, and soon there were over 5000 men, and as many women and children. It was mid afternoon and the disciples quickly grew concerned that the people would soon be getting hungry as most of them had come a long way. I told them to give the people something to eat, and I asked Philip where we should buy bread. Philip laughed and exclaimed with a great good humoured snort, 'Why it would require two hundred days wages, for just a little for each!' Andrew, who could always find the beginning of a thread, said, 'This small boy has five loaves and two fishes, but what are these among so many?' It was springtime, so I had the disciples tell the multitude to seat themselves on the lush green grass that was over the land. So they sat down in groups of 50 and 100. I took the loaves with the two fish, and I looked up to the heavens and asked my father to bless this food. Then I began breaking it up and giving pieces to the disciples so they could put the food in baskets and distribute it to the people, and there was enough. I told the disciples to gather what remained, that nothing be wasted.

After the crowd had eaten they began to talk, for they knew what had happened, and they planned together to lift me up and make me king. I saw what they had in mind, and although their intentions may have been good, these people had no authority to make me king, and such an act would only have lead to disaster, when word of such a thing reached Jerusalem and Rome. I dismissed the crowd and ordered the disciples to go to the boat and cast off for Capernaum. Knowing the people would not accept my dismissal, I cloaked myself and went to the top of the mountain. Just before dawn I looked out over the sea, with the moon being bright as it waxed toward the full moon of the upcoming Passover. The wind was strong over the water, and I saw the boat heading against the waves. All twelve were rowing with difficulty, and they were making no progress. It was about three miles to their position, and I walked down the mountain and out over the sea toward them. I continued walking past the boat, and when they saw me they exclaimed out in fright, thinking I was an apparition. I called out to them to have no fear, as it was I they saw. Peter quickly stood up and said. "Lord, if it is you, command me to come to you over the waters." "Come,"[54] I said. Peter immediately came out of the boat and began walking over the water toward me, but, feeling the windstorm, he became afraid and began to sink. I was proud of Peter, but was in no way inclined to give him praise for giving up certainty in an act of faith before it was complete, so I corrected him for his giving way to doubt, and I pulled him from the water. Together we walked to the boat and boarded it. After we were aboard the wind subsided, and I mildly instructed the men to continue on our way, for they were frozen by the events, not knowing whether to be afraid or exuberant. My words broke the spell and after glancing quickly at each other, with nervous grins and whispered comments about my being, indeed, the Son of God, they quickly returned to the task of rowing. We soon came to Gennesaret, where James and John's parents lived. After anchoring the boat, we made our way to the shore, where we relaxed and ate from the leftovers of the previous evening. The disciples were numb, in a kind of euphoria. They had come face to face with such tangible proof of the power of things spiritual that, even though their minds had already believed in the truth of such things, they were overloaded with faith, not knowing if they were in a dream and would soon wake up, or what would happen next. It was only a short time before we were seen, and many people came to us, bringing their sick, who were cured, and the men fell into a routine more familiar to them, the events of the last few hours slipping into the manageable confines of memory.

When we reached Capernaum much of the crowd that had been with us the night before came to us, and they were indignant that we had left them, asking us when we had arrived back. I admonished them, for I knew that they merely wanted us to feed them again, so they asked me, "What must we do to do the works God requires?" "The work of God is this," I said, "to believe in the one he has sent." [55] But the crowd was not satisfied, and they asked what sign

I would perform, so that they could see it and believe in me.

It was at this point that the two main streams of activity in my life since my baptism began to merge. I had been teaching the people, and I had been trying to reason with the priests. I saw that in terms of teaching the great crowds of people I really could go no further, because to do so I would have to assume the role of God's appointed leader, in the tradition of Moses, allowing them to lift me up as their king, and accept the role. To do so without the blessing of the priests would have been an act of presumption on my part, an act against God himself, for the rulers of the nation had been ordained by his law. As a descendent of David I had a right to be made the King of Israel, but to become this I would need to be sanctified by the anointed priests of God, through their recognition of the will of God and their acting in His name.

This did not mean that I would stop teaching the people of the land, if for no other reason than my disciples needed to gain experience in teaching so that when I was gone they would be able to continue the Work, with or without the priesthood. But I saw clearly that my ability to keep the good faith of the average man would now begin to diminish unless progress was made with the men of power.

Seeing these underlying forces at work, I was not surprised when the crowd pointed out, disputing my admonition that all they wanted was food, that Moses did give the people heavenly bread, the manna in the wilderness. Since I was now aware that this interchange had taken on a new dimension—the convergence of the parallel avenues of teaching now limiting my ability to influence the people—I was prepared to answer them directly, as I would the Pharisees, and I pointed out that manna was not truly a heavenly thing, being fabricated from the natural things of the earth, and that God, not Moses, had given it to them. And since the question was to the point, I continued by saying that God indeed had given them the bread from heaven, and this was the One that had come down to them from heaven to give life to the world. 'Lord, always give us that bread,' [56] the people responded.

There was no reason to turn back, and I said point blank, that I was that bread. I continued to say that he who came to me would not get hungry at all, and the one who believed in me would not get thirsty at all. But they had seen me and still did not believe, I told them. I explained that the Father had given me the world, and thus this world would one day become mine, with the ability to give life; also I would not reject anyone who came to me. I had come to earth at this time to do the will of God, and this was his will, that I lose nothing out of this world, but I should resurrect it all at the last day. For the will of God was that everyone who understood me and exercised faith in me should have everlasting life.

After I said these things the crowd began to grow agitated, saying things like, 'Is this not Jesus, the son of Joseph?' [57] But I told them to stop murmuring, and I continued to say that no man could believe in me unless God allowed it through spirit, and the ones that did believe me I would resurrect at the beginning of the new world. I pointed out that the prophets promised, 'They will all be taught by God,' and I continued to explain that everyone who had looked for God and learned from God would come to me. I further told them that no one had seen God except the one that came from God, and that I was telling the truth when I said he that believed, he would get everlasting life by believing.

I did not stop, and I reminded them that their forefathers ate manna in the wilderness, but they died, but that here is bread that comes from heaven, so that if a man eats this bread he will not die. And I ended by saying, "I am the living bread that came down from heaven. If anyone eats of this bread, he will live forever. This bread is my flesh, which I will give for the life of the world." [58]

This was enough and the crowd dispersed thinking and muttering.

The next day was the Sabbath and I went to the synagogue to take part in the service and to talk, as was now my custom when I was in Capernaum. I knew that regardless of what I said my progress with the people at large had reached its apex. The true conflict was now taking place in the spiritual world between Satan, acting through the men who ruled in God's name but lay under the power of darkness, and the Spirit of God as it manifested through me, and to a lesser degree, my followers. So I did not hold back, but spoke to the matter that was in everyone's heart. I began, saying, "I tell you the truth, unless you eat the flesh of the Son of Man and drink his blood, you have no life in you."[59]

The reaction of the crowd was bad, to say the least. Was I a priest of darkness, to talk of drinking blood and eating human flesh?

It was abundantly evident, from the nature of our religion, from the nature of all of my actions on the earth, and from the symbolic and sacred nature of bread and blood throughout our scriptures, not to mention simple common sense, that what I had said was simply a metaphor. But the perversity of the reaction to my words was actually as understandable as the reaction of the Pharisees to my healing on the Sabbath, or the elders of Nazareth attempting to take my life, so I was not concerned that the metaphor I used was open to base interpretations, because the people would understand or not based on the condition of their hearts. And despite their directness, the words were the absolute truth.

Of course the symbols of blood and bread are everyday terms today, although still not well understood. Even some of my disciples made no effort to understand, but concurred with the general feelings of the crowd that this sort of speech was shocking, and saying, "This is a hard teaching. Who can accept it?" [60]

The moment of truth continued with some further words and further reactions. Many of my disciples left, and did not continue to follow me.

I turned to the twelve and asked, 'You do not want to leave too, do you?' [61] Peter replied, "Lord, to whom shall we go? You have the words of eternal life. We believe and know that you are the Holy One of God." [62] The twelve remained, but I saw that Judas had stumbled.

For all men the Truth can be a difficult thing and Satan will try every man. Those on earth today who think that my teachings will bring about only kindness and compassion in their life should remember my sayings:

"No servant is greater than his master. If they persecuted me, they will persecute you also. If they obeyed my teaching, they will obey yours also. They will treat you this way because of my name, for they do not know the One who sent me." [63]

And:

"Do you think I came to bring peace on earth? No, I tell you, but division. From now on there will be five in one family divided against each other, three against two and two against three. They will be divided, father against son and son against father, mother against daughter and daughter against mother, mother-in-law against daughter-in-law and daughter-in-law against mother-in-law." [64]

# CHAPTER NINE

---

Within the week we left for Jerusalem and the Passover to continue with what was now The Work—engaging the Pharisees. The trip was fruitless, however, for I had to be cautious, as everywhere my life was in danger. None the less, we spent the festival in the holy city, and it was important to me that my disciples and I be there together on that night. I would not give up trying to turn the minds of the Pharisees, but it was not my time to die. After the days were over, we returned to Galilee and continued our efforts to teach and heal.

Many scribes and Pharisees from Jerusalem followed us to Capernaum, looking for grounds on which to accuse me of breaking the law. They would twist the law to try and make my actions or words appear to be a violation of the Law of Moses. But what grounds they found only sprang from their own traditions, and spirit deflected the accusations. The rules and traditions that had been written down over the last handful of generations had begun to make a mockery of the law, which more than anything else they now used as an instrument of power for their own benefit. The law no longer had very much to do with God, for they worshipped God with their lips, but their hearts were far from Him. What they held up to be the Doctrine of the Truth was in fact little more than the commands of men, used to exert and hold power over other men. Perhaps for many of the leaders the progress to this state of corruption had been made with the best of intentions, 'for the good of the people.' The intoxication that occurs when men experience the power that comes from exerting what is, in the beginning, genuine spiritual authority is apparently irresistible to most. It is Satan's most effective weapon in his battle against the Truth, and there is not a religion on the face of the earth that has not fallen prey to this corruption. The reason this corruption is so insidious is that it appears in the form of righteousness. When a man becomes acquainted with the fact that God exists, and, in fact lives in the same moment as he, himself, he wants to exert all his strength to come closer to God, to please God. He does good works and is acknowledged by his fellow man. He disciplines himself and becomes strong in his habits. These men come naturally to leadership. The problem is that the dilemma of the earth is more complex than simply mastering a few of the most obvious obstacles that face us all. And one of the complexities that ensure our continued enslavement to being and doing wrong is that time is a real and unrelenting part of our lives. The path seems clear for a man who begins to understand God and finds some happiness in extricating himself from the most obvious snares that face us all. But as time passes the man becomes concerned that others have not mastered their own natures as well as he has. These other men now appear to be in the way of his happiness, in the way of the happiness of the earth, and most to the point, in God's way. This creates a natural conflict, and the trap is that the easy answer to this conflict seems to be found in the need to change the behaviour of the other men. After all, this appears to be what God wants. Since these disciplined men are often leaders, they find an ally in men like themselves, all seeking to control others, which they mistakenly think is the will of God. Such a simple thing. It is not a credit to mankind that the dark forces have been able to use this simple half truth to manipulate men with such ease that any real movement toward God on the part of an expanding group of sincere men can easily be transformed into a debacle. The well intentioned leaders are quickly transformed from seekers and sowers of truth to sowers of division and hatred. In the defence of such men it can be said that their strong desire for a simple and straightforward path to deliverance is a worthy master, but that is merely another half truth, and does nothing to save the man using such logic from the fact that he has fallen from the Path. The gift of purity and discipline is given by God to all men who seek it with sincerity and effort and prayer, but it is its own reward. When the goodness of a man leads to his resentment of others, it is time to return to the beginning, to humility and solitude. Being strong in the knowledge of God's law is never an excuse for allowing oneself to indulge in the sin of judging another man in the name of God. But such is the nature and strength of the dark spirit that rules the earth that man is easily turned against his fellow man, and no iniquity or act of violence or unthinking cruelty is too great to be perpetuated in the name of God.

This is what I faced.

The disciples were exhausted by the unreasoning and unrelenting opposition of the leaders of our religion, and for a fact, so was I. After some discussion we planned a trip that would afford us time to relax and build up strength, and enjoy ourselves. We headed for the regions of Tyre and Sidon, some miles to the north. I instructed the men to keep our whereabouts secret. In all the time we taught, this was the only trip we made outside the land of Israel. We paid for the use of a house near Sidon, and after a refreshing stay we headed south again, on foot, then east across the headwaters of the Jordan to the region of Decapolis. Although this was primarily a gentile area, many hundreds and then thousands of Jews came to hear us and to be taught. Once again the crowds became large, and when they were running out of food, for many had been with us in the countryside for two or three days, I felt sorry for them and fed them. But such miraculous food was not the object of the message I had to give, so we travelled once again to the Sea of

Galilee, where we boarded a boat and crossed over to the western shore, hoping to return to Capernaum. But immediately we were encountered by a large group of Pharisees and Sadducees from Jerusalem, who demanded that I perform a great sign for them as a signal of my authenticity. There was neither goodness of intention nor room for truth in their minds, so I warned them that they were a wicked generation, and that the only sign they would see was the sign of Jonah, which I used to represent the three days I would spend in the bowels of the earth before I was resurrected, just as Jonah had spent three days in the stomach of the fish before he was disgorged.

We returned to the boat and headed for the northeast tip of the sea, to a place known as Bethsaida. From there we headed north, at the direction of spirit, toward the district of Caesarea Philippi. Here the land slopes continually upward until it comes to an area high above the rest of the countryside. It was only about thirty miles from the water, but the continual ascent made for slow walking, and the climb took us two days. I was now certain that my death was not far off, and so I was pensive, wanting to make sure I had left nothing unsaid or undone between the twelve and myself. On the way I instructed Peter about things that were to come, and I entrusted him to begin the New Congregation that I would establish on the earth, for I also knew with some assurance that Israel was to be cut off, and teaching would have to go on without the Great Organization of the Living God, without the Religion of the Priests of Judah. I knew it was time to tell the disciples in plain words that I was going to face suffering and death at the hands of the Jews. They did not accept it well, for they knew I had power to avoid death at the hands of men, and they could not understand why I would choose to allow such a thing to happen. Everything we had done on our great adventure pointed to a happy ending by the reckonings of men and their fables, and although this was to be ultimately true, they never really understood why it had to be the way it was, until I brought them understanding from the other side of death. A number of my close followers had joined us on the trek to the mountain and I had time to warn them, as we walked, that to follow me was a difficult path, and that they should be prepared to leave everything behind, even life itself, if they chose to continue following me.

I could see the distress of my disciples as they struggled to understand why I must be put to death, especially Peter and John, who I think in some way felt that they must have let me down, that perhaps they could have done, or do, something to alter this unhappy fate. I could have tried harder, I suppose, to explain the necessity of what was to happen, but I did not. The truth is that the full understanding of the sacred secret was not to become fully clear, even, in a sense, to me, until after I was resurrected. My death had the potential to free the ultimate destiny of mankind from the grip of death and slavery forever. But as we walked toward the mountain this thing had not occurred. I still had to reach the point of death and be worthy of resurrection by God, and this meant that should I make a mistake, any mistake at all, between any moment along my path and the final second of my life, I would have accomplished nothing except a lot of magical things and a lot of talk, none of which would have helped mankind one iota in the long run. We would have had to start over with some other plan to save the earth. As the Son of God, I was going to succeed, but Satan is powerful on the earth, and had he known exactly what was going on, he may well have acted very differently than he did to the increased suffering and despair of the world. The sacred secret was to remain just that, a secret, until all things were complete. And so the complete understanding of it was veiled by spirit until its completion, from every living creature except God. This was not a play that the disciples and I simply walked through, this was the Living Moment of the True Universal Reality, and as such, on the earth, the next moment was primarily based on the choices and actions of the one before. Just as God did not will the fall of the earth, so He could not simply will the deliverance of earth. It had to be earned, as it had been lost, by action. Any slip on my part could mean all was lost.

But I did now know, with the full power of my being, what I should do at every moment, and it was only a few moments later that I separated John and Peter and James from the others and proceeded to walk with them toward the top of Mount Hermon.

It was almost dusk when we began making our way up the side of the mountain. Spirit allowed me to make sure that that the weather was perfect, although I did not do this consciously. As we climbed, our thoughts became linked to our ascent, the journey growing more and more spiritual as we went. Our concentration filtered out the noise of baser thought and shook off any collected bits of doubt or confusion. A stumble and a quick look down reminded us to clear our minds of any lack of faith, and allow spirit to guide our climb. It was about midnight when we reached as high as we were going to go, and the three each found a place to sit, a place to catch their breath and gaze around at the beauty of the heights. I went a few paces away to my own spot and after looking about, I began to pray.

I had been in prayer for a while when I felt spirit increase its intensity within me. I opened my eyes to see that my body was shining with a bright white light. I stood up and as I did the disciples sat up, for they had been falling asleep. My entire body was now replaced by light, although my form stayed intact, and I was intensely alive, as if I was in the higher worlds. As I turned my head I saw two equally bright figures, and I recognized them to be angels, although they appeared in the form of Moses and Elijah. I knew they were not the actual prophets for they remained in the common grave of mankind until the day I was to call them out, but they explained to me that for the sake of my followers they would appear as symbols they knew. The angels began to talk to me about my departure, by which they meant my upcoming death, and this also was for the benefit of the three, that they might see and know that my death would neither be an end nor something to be avoided, but a time of great spiritual fulfillment. As they moved away, Peter hurried over to ask if he could prepare a tent for each of us. I almost laughed, and if my smile could have been brighter than the light of which I was composed, it would have been. At that moment a luminous fog surrounded us and the voice of God was heard, "This is my Son, whom I love; with him I am well pleased. Listen to him!" [65] I looked again to the three, and they were on the ground in fear, so I went to them and raised them up and told them not to be afraid, but at peace. We spent the rest of the night on the mountain. The fog had disappeared with the angels, so we slept under the bright sky. The stars seemed immediate, and living, as if to remind us of the nature of the light of which I had only a few minutes before been composed. The disciples rested in a kind of euphoria. I was at peace as well, for I knew that spirit had provided a rare and transcendent moment that was not only for the benefit of the Teaching that was to come, and the fulfillment of Scripture, but also gave my friends a living memory that would ease their pain in a way that the best of words could not.

In the morning we walked down to the camp of my followers, which was near a small town at the base of the mountain. As we approached the town we could see that there was something wrong. My disciples were there, arguing with a group of scribes, and as I approached I asked them what the dispute was about. The townsfolk had brought a boy to my disciples to be cured. This boy had been possessed of a demon since childhood, and although they tried, my disciples had not been able to dispel it. The scribes were delighting in this failure, and were busy criticizing the friends. "O unbelieving generation," I said, "how long shall I stay with you? How long shall I put up with you?"[66] I said this for the benefit of the scribes. I had asked the boy's father to bring him to me, but as the youth approached the demon who possessed him threw him to the ground in a great convulsion. I questioned the father, who was appealing to me with great urgency, and with great faith. I threw out the demon and revived the boy, who was exhausted to the point of death. When the boy's father had been begging me for help he had asked me if I could, indeed, help. I had responded that all things can be for one who has faith, to which he said, "I do believe; help me overcome my unbelief!" [67] This was a wise thing for him to say, and in a way it answered the question of why the disciples had not been able to cure the boy. Later when they asked me why they were unable to do this thing, when they had done such things before, I explained to them that this was a very powerful spirit, and that they should have resorted to prayer to strengthen their own faith. Once again I stressed that faith is the key to all works, and added that increasing faith is a work of its own.

I wished to return home to Capernaum, and on the way I made certain that we went unnoticed. I wanted to make it clear to the men what was going to happen in the near future, for although I was sure of these things they were still resisting knowing. So I said directly, "The Son of Man is going to be betrayed into the hands of men. They will kill him, and on the third day he will be raised to life." [68] Even after that they were unclear on the matter, but they were afraid to question me about it further, so I said no more and we continued on our way to Capernaum.

The wind of spirit had shifted, and the land lay quiet, as if watching to see what might become of me. My disciples and I had time to sit and meditate and reflect on things in a traditional way. We discussed many things, the things of human nature, the little things that had been put aside in the intense and relentless Work we had been doing. The disciples squabbled about who among them was the greatest, and I corrected them for missing the point that in al

150

likelihood the least of men on this world had the best chance of being correct in the True Reality. I also reminded them of what they knew full well from meditation, that one has to be innocent and receptive to have union with spirit. It was important for us to talk about this kind of thing, for when I was gone so would be the great spiritual center that kept those around me from slipping back to the limits set by the mundane trials all men go through on a daily basis. I gave them guidelines concerning how to deal with their fellow men, knowing they would pass such advice on to those they were to teach in the coming years.

It was a peaceful time, perhaps a small gift from my Father. Even my brothers came to visit me from Nazareth. Although they still did not understand that I was the Son of Man, as they all would eventually, they nonetheless wanted me to succeed in what they perceived was my attempt to become famous. With this in mind they urged me to go to Jerusalem for the upcoming Festival of Tabernacles, thinking our temporarily quiet time was a waste of time, pointing out, "No one who wants to become a public figure acts in secret." [69] They were not aware of the gravity of the situation, and I insisted my disciples make nothing known to them or my mother about what was to occur. But I did respond to them that I was hated by the world because I made it known that its works were wicked, and I told them to go ahead with the travelling parties about to leave for Jerusalem. Several days later the disciples and I left for the Festival without telling anyone, taking the less travelled route through Samaria, as I had done on my trip to the temple when I was young.

It had now been three years since John had baptized me, and many things had taken place. At the Festival the crowds were wondering about me, asking, 'Where is that man?'[70] and debating about who I was; some insisting I was a good man and others certain that I was misleading them. And yet no man spoke out publicly in my favor, even those who had been cured, for they were in fear of the anger of the priests.

The Festival of Tabernacles is the great harvest feast. It is a time of great rejoicing for the people and lasts for seven days. We arrived about half way through the celebrations, and immediately made our way to the temple. I began to teach, and I spoke for quite a long time, and the crowd received my words well. Many of the crowd were travellers from throughout all Israel and the lands around, as was the case at all festivals, and they did not know that the rulers had planned to kill me. Despite this I talked about the Pharisees desiring my death, which confused many, but I wanted to make one all important point, and it related to my persecution, and that was to "Stop judging by mere appearances, and make a right judgment." [71] The world, to this day, has not listened to this.

Although the visitors to the city knew nothing of the plans against me, the people of Judea did, and they wondered if the fact that I had not been captured might mean that the rulers had accepted that I was the Christ. Now the Pharisees were trying hard to convince the people of Judea that I could not be the Christ, and one method they used was to stress that I was a Galilean, for the Judeans had a saying, 'Nothing good can come out of Galilee.' The Pharisees knew that I had been born in Bethlehem, but they kept this from the people to serve their own purposes. When the crowd of Judeans began to challenge me on this, albeit without scriptural correctness, asking how a Galilean could be the Anointed One, I responded with the truth. After clarifying the prophecies that related to their questions, I added that the real problem was that they did not know God, which infuriated them, and they tried to seize me to take me to the authorities, but I escaped.

Despite the hostility generated by those who hated me, many came to have faith in me, and pointed out all that I had done, saying. "When the Christ comes, will he do more miraculous signs than this man?" [72] When the Pharisees heard the people saying this sort of thing they immediately sent out soldiers to arrest me. I knew this but I kept on speaking. There were several incidents. When the soldiers would arrive they would listen to me, and on seeing the crowd also listening, they would not arrest me, for they themselves were not certain in their hearts that I was not the Christ, and they would avoid arresting me, saying to each other that it was not a good time, and so it went. On the seventh day of the festival I was still preaching on the steps of the temple, and I explained to the people, with great emotion and spirit, who I was and why I had come, and I offered them the water of life. Many accepted me, but others did not, and disputes arose as I spoke. The soldiers who had come again still could not find it in their hearts to arrest me, and they returned to the Pharisees and the chief priests. The priests were in great anger when they saw that I had not been captured, and they chastised the soldiers, and they would not listen to anyone, even from among themselves, who would speak in my defence, so great was their hatred.

After the soldiers had left I proceeded deeper into the temple, to the court of women, which is the innermost court allowing women and children, and continued to teach. On each night of the festival it was in this sanctuary that four massive lampstands were placed and lit. Each lampstand was supplied by four huge basins of oil, so that the light was immense, illuminating not only the temple, but the whole vicinity. Even here the Pharisees challenged me, and this continued throughout the evening and the next day. Most of the next day was spent in such argument, for I was earnestly trying to reason with them, but to no avail. Finally they became enraged, and picked up stones to hurl at me, but I hid from them and left the temple

Although the festival was over we did not leave Jerusalem, but decided to stay through the next Sabbath. It was on the Sabbath that we were walking through the city when Andrew noticed a boy who had been blind since birth, and asked me who had sinned, the boy or his parents? He asked this because many rabbis taught that a child could sin in the womb. I told him that neither the boy nor his parents had sinned, but that in this case his infirmity was going to become involved in the working out of the will of God. To cure the boy I used a ritual that would be familiar to him and give him faith, and when he returned from the Pool of Siloam, as I had so instructed, he could see. He began to rejoice and would not stop, and some of his neighbours did not believe that it was him, thinking, 'this is a man who looks like him.' When they realized it was the same boy, they took him to their synagogue and told the Pharisees what had happened. The Pharisees asked the boy what had happened, but upon hearing they said of me, "This man is not from God, for he does not keep the Sabbath." Well, the neighbours asked them, "Why not?" and the Pharisees replied, "Because he does not observe the Sabbath."[73] But some of the Pharisees wondered how a man could do such things and not be a man of God, and they were divided. So they asked the boy what he thought and the boy replied, "He is a prophet." [74] But they could not believe this, thinking there was some kind of plot between the boy and me, so they summoned the boy's parents.

The boy's parents knew that anyone expressing faith in me would be expelled from the synagogue, and that the cutting off of such fellowship amounted to exclusion from the community at large, which could spell disaster for this poor couple, so they were very cautious. The Pharisees asked them if this was their son who had been born blind, and if it was, how was it that he now saw? The parents replied that yes, this was their son who had been born blind, but they did not want to say they knew why he could now see, so they asked the Pharisees to ask the boy himself, pointing out that he was of age. So the Pharisees called the boy again and tried to intimidate him, saying they had evidence that I was a sinner, and they demanded that the boy give glory to God. The boy replied boldly, for he had been a beggar all his life and was used to being pushed around, "Whether he is a sinner or not, I don't know. One thing I do know. I was blind but now I see!" [75] The Pharisees wanted to find a flaw in the boy's story, so they asked him again what I had done to restore his sight. The boy, being who he was, replied, "I have told you already and you did not listen. Why do you want to hear it again?" and added, for his own pleasure, "Do you want to become his disciples, too?"[76] Of course the Pharisees were enraged and they hurled insults at him and said, "You are this fellow's disciple! We are disciples of Moses! We know that God spoke to Moses, but as for this fellow, we don't even know where he comes from." [77] Now, as I said, this boy was not afraid of men, for they had done all they could to him, so he spoke his mind, which was a good one, "Now that is remarkable! You don't know where he comes from, yet he opened my eyes. We know that God does not listen to sinners. He listens to the Godly man who does his will. Nobody has ever heard of opening the eyes of a man born blind. If this man were not from God, he could do nothing." To this they replied, "You were steeped in sin at birth; how dare you lecture us!" And they threw him out,[78] expelling him from the synagogue.

When I learned what they had done to the boy, I sought him out, and I asked him, "Do you believe in the son of man?" [79] And he said, "Who is he, sir?[80] Tell me so that I may believe in him."[81] I replied, "You have now seen him; in fact, he is the one speaking to you."[82] The boy bowed before me, and said with all sweetness, "I do put faith in him, Lord."[83] I then said for the sake of the Pharisees who were listening, "For this judgement I came into this world: that those not seeing might see and those seeing might become blind."[84] The Pharisees immediately said, "What? Are we blind too?"[85] I wanted them to know the difference between the sins that are made simply from human weakness, and the sin that is made with a hardened mind, so I said, "If you were blind, you would not be guilty of sin, but now that you claim that you can see, your guilt remains." [86]

# CHAPTER TEN

———————— ❧ ————————

When we left Jerusalem we did not head home to Galilee, but remained in the countryside around the capital. The great majority of my teaching had been in Galilee, so I determined to stay in Judea and focus our attention there, and on Perea, which lay on the east side of the Jordan, for the people there had not had much chance to hear us.

I called all my disciples to me, and there were about two hundred, and of these I chose seventy. I divided the seventy into groups of two, and I sent them out ahead of us, wherever we planned to go. I gave them the power, and I instructed them, to cure the sick.

When the followers began to return to me, they reported all that had happened. They were filled with surprise and happiness at what they had accomplished. "Lord, even the demons submit to us in your name," [87] they would say, and I was made to know everything that had been done. When they had all come in I felt a great joy, for I knew that even after I left the earth the teaching was secure and would be continued with the power of spirit, and would succeed. I prayed to my father, expressing my great gratitude for what He had allowed, and I was again filled with joy and the power of the spirit, and turning to my disciples I said to them, "Blessed are the eyes that see what you see. For I tell you that many prophets and kings wanted to see what you see but did not see it, and to hear what you hear but did not hear it." [88] I was, truthfully, a little surprised at the great things these simple and humble people had achieved, for the twelve had not gone with them, so I spoke to them, "I praise you, Father, Lord of heaven and earth, because you have hidden these things from the wise and learned, and revealed them to little children. Yes, Father, for this was your good pleasure."[89] The spirit was brightly alive in the earth, but it was not from me that the great energy came, my disciples and my followers were the source of this power, because I had granted it to them. I realized that no one would get this great knowledge without the granting of it by the One my father had sent to the world, and I was doubly happy, for I now knew the Teachings could not be defeated, even by the dark one himself.

After this a change came to my teaching, for I became drawn to Jerusalem, and I could not look away. And I began to tell all the things I wanted my disciples to know, and that I wanted recorded in scripture, because I knew I did not have much time.

I began a slow spiral toward Jerusalem and the fulfillment of my work. I would approach the city and I would move away, seeing the time was not right. I would withdraw, only to approach again. And many Pharisees would come out to challenge me and to test me and to try to catch me up, but it was not entirely of their own volition, for they had been moved to do and say these things so that I might issue the last warnings to Israel, and that I might prophecy regarding the things that were to come regarding the end of God's singular relationship with Israel, and the beginning of a new Chosen People, to be taken from all the nations of the earth.

I made appearances in all the villages around Jerusalem, in Jericho and in Bethany and in Bethphage, and my disciples and I would go past Bethany to the Mount of Olives, and we would withdraw. And all the time I would issue warnings to Israel, and speak metaphors concerning the things to come. I was very troubled, for I was a Jew, and like all Jews I longed for the day that Israel and God would be united in a time of joy and prosperity, and I could see that this was not to be. My heart broke for the Nation, and I suffered that I could not reach out to them and bring them to me, and give them the glory and the riches of the kingdom of heaven. I continued to go around and into Jerusalem, but each time we came into danger, and yet it was not the time, so we withdrew. Finally, I went off to pray by myself, and it was given to me that we should depart. The next day we began to travel, and we headed north and crossed over the Jordan into the area of Perea. After a time we came to the spot where John used to baptize, and this is where we made camp, for I had been directed to come here. It had been almost three and a half years since I had made my way out of the pool I now gazed down upon. The memories flooded over me, remembering how I had been filled with the spirit of the kingdom of the heavens as I emerged from the water, and how my very presence shook the foundations of the earth with the power of the knowledge of God. I was quiet, and soon the memories joined with the present. I was heavy with emotion as I reviewed all that had happened since that day, but I prayed, and the sorrow and the sweetness subsided. I walked back to the camp in a kind of numbness, a kind of emptiness.

Soon the people of the surrounding towns became aware of us, and they began to come to us, to see, and to bring their sick, and we cured them. Many of them came to believe that I was the Son of God, for they knew that John had not preformed a single miracle, but that he had foretold my coming.

We also travelled to some of the out of the way places around our camp, and we were in such a place, a nearby village, when a man came stumbling into the room, exhausted from his journey. He had brought word that Lazarus the brother of Mary was sick. Now I had come to know Mary, the woman who had washed my feet with her tears, after she had returned to Bethany as I had instructed her. She had remained in Bethany with her sister Martha and her brother Lazarus ever since. They had all become believers, and were devoted to me, so that we often stayed with them when we were in the vicinity of Jerusalem. Lazarus was a good man, slight, and with the features considered classic to my people. He was a man with a quiet self assurance that sprung, I think, from an irresistible sense of humor. I had become very fond of him, as I had his sisters. Martha was strikingly beautiful, and equally strong, with untiring energy and competence that she put to the task of seeing to the needs of others. Of all the people on the earth, next to my family and the twelve, it was these three that knew me best as a man.

We gave the messenger something to eat and I reassured him, telling him to rest and return to Bethany. Two days went by and then I said to the disciples, 'Let us go back into Judea.'[90] They were amazed, and said, "A short while ago the Jews tried to stone you, and yet you are going back there?" [91] They said this because they were content with the peace of where we were, but I explained to them that there was a time to do things and a time not to, and that this was a time to do things, and then I hinted to them about Lazarus, but they did not understand, so I said clearly, "Lazarus is dead..."[92] They became dejected, but Thomas soon stood and began to prepare for the trip, saying, with a note of resigned humor, "Let us also go, that we may die with him,"[93] referring to the danger that awaited me if I returned to Jerusalem.

We arrived at Bethany without incident, and Lazarus had been in the tomb four days, having died even as the messenger was returning. As we approached the house Martha came out to meet me, and said, "Lord, if you had been here my brother would not have died. But I know that even now God will give you whatever you ask." I said to her: "Your brother will rise again" and she replied, "I know he will rise again in the resurrection at the last day," and I said to her, "I am the resurrection and the life. He who believes in me will live, even though he dies; and whoever lives and believes in me will never die. Do you believe this?" She said,

"Yes, Lord, I believe that you are the Christ, the Son of God, who was to come into the world." [94] I asked her to get Mary for me, and she returned to the house, and I waited for them. Many people had gathered at their house to offer their sorrow and to help, and when Mary ran out to come to me, they had followed her.

When Mary reached me, she fell to the ground and said, "Lord, if you had been here, my brother would not have died." [95] When I saw her, and Martha, and the people who had come out with her, I was struck, for they were all weeping, and I felt a great pressure of sorrow rise within me, ignoring my thoughts, which knew that all would be well. I said, "Where have you laid him?" [96] And they began to lead me to him, but as we went I gave way to tears, for I could not control myself, but I heard some of the people say, "See, how he loved him!"[97] But others said: "Could not he who opened the eyes of the blind man have kept this man from dying?"[98] As we approached the Memorial tomb I again felt spirit groan within me, but I took strength and I ordered them to take away the rock that closed the mouth of the tomb, and I brought Lazarus to life. When he came out they unwrapped him, and his skin was like that of a young man.

Many of the people who had come to console Mary and Martha were from Jerusalem, which was only a few miles away, and so news of the resurrection came quickly to the Pharisees. When the high priests heard the news they and the Pharisees summoned the Sanhedrin, the high court of the Jews, and they reasoned that the people may take faith in me as a whole, and they were afraid of their positions and of the reactions of Rome, so after they conferred, they decided that I should be put to death. After that time I could no longer walk about in public, so my disciples and I fled to Ephraim, which was near the wilderness, and we stayed there.

As the Passover approached, I knew that the time had come, and

I could wait no longer. I gathered the twelve and we left Ephraim, heading in a great circle north up into Galilee, then east across the Jordan into Perea and following the river south until we crossed over again, heading for Jerusalem and the final day. As we began to head south toward Judea we were joined on the road by great parties of travelling Jews, all heading for Jerusalem as we were. I healed everyone who came to us with a disease, the blind and the deaf, the lepers and the ones with twisted limbs. And I spoke as we went, sometimes arguing with angry Pharisees, sometimes confiding with my disciples whatever they could hear, and all these things may be read about me. We passed through Jericho, and there was a great throng that followed us out of the city up the long climb toward Jerusalem.

When we reached Bethany, there were but six days until the Passover. Martha knew that we were coming and she had arranged for a great evening meal for my disciples and me. There were to be many in attendance, and so Martha had arranged to have the meal at the home of a man named Simon, who was wealthy, but faithful, being a leper that I had cured. It was an elaborate meal and, as was usually the case, Martha was occupied with all the things that needed to be done, while Mary sat near me listening and watching that I would need for nothing. Early in the dinner, as we were reclining, Mary brought out a flask of oil and began to apply it to my feet and to my head, drying my feet with her hair as she had done when I first met her at the house of the Pharisee in Nain. Now this oil was precious, being worth about a year's wages and it was extremely beautiful, the intoxicating scent filling the whole room. As was often the case, Mary came under criticism for her attention to me and for her lack of concern for anything else. This time the objection came from my disciples, who were embarrassed by this extravagant gesture, and spoke up saying, 'Why this waste?' for she seemed determined to use the entire flask, which would be almost a pound. Judas added to the concern by saying 'Why is it this perfumed oil was not sold for three hundred denarii and given to the poor people?'[99] I came to Mary's defence by saying, "Let her alone. Why do you try to make trouble for her? She did a fine deed toward me. For you always have the poor with you, and whenever you want to you can always do them good, but me you do not have always. She did what she could: she undertook beforehand to put perfumed oil on my body in view of the burial."[100] (Now by this I meant payment for the resurrection of Lazarus) Truly I say to you, wherever the good news is preached in all the world, what this woman did shall also be told as a remembrance of her."[101] And they all let her alone.

Within a few hours the Pharisees learned about this dinner, and they decided they would kill Lazarus as well as me, for he represented a sign that the people could not ignore.

It was early Sunday morning, by the calendar of the modern world, and there were only five periods of daylight before the Passover meal that would take place Thursday night. My disciples and I left Bethany and proceeded over the Mount of Olives toward Jerusalem. It was only a few miles to Jerusalem, and as we came over the hill and looked down on Bethphage, which nestled on the eastern slope of the mountain, I sent John and Philip into the town. I told them they would come upon an ass, with a young colt beside her, tied to a railing. I instructed them to untie the animals and bring them to me, and that if anyone stopped them, they were to say, 'The Lord needs them.'[102] They said this thing to the men who questioned them, and they allowed the disciples to go on their way. The disciples did not realize it at the time, but these things occurred so that the prophecy of Zechariah, the prophet, might be fulfilled. For he said, "Rejoice greatly, O Daughter of Zion! Shout, Daughter of Jerusalem! See, your king comes to you, righteous and having salvation, gentle and riding on a donkey, on a colt, the foal of a donkey."[103] But it was a sad moment for me, because I knew that Jerusalem would receive me with bitterness underlying the jubilation.

As I placed my outer robe on the back of the colt, the disciples spread their own on the mother, as they would not be less than their master in humility, and I began to ride the colt toward the city. As we grew closer, the crowds were gathering in front of us, and they began to throw their outer robes onto the path before me, and to cut palm branches and strew them along the way. The people began to cry out, "Blessed is the king who comes in the name of the Lord!" and, "Peace in heaven and glory in the highest!"[104] Some of the Pharisees complained to me to rebuke my followers, but I said to them, "I tell you, if they keep quiet, the stones will cry out." [105]

As we drew near Jerusalem the morning sun was full on the city, and the temple shone like a jewel. It reminded my of my first sight of the city when I was a boy, and emotion rose within me so that I could not help but begin to cry, knowing what might have been. And I reasoned to myself, yet I spoke all things out loud. "Jerusalem, if you, even you, had only known on this day what would bring you peace—but now it is hidden from your eyes."[106] And spirit rose within me so that I spoke a prophecy that was bitter to my tongue. "The days will come upon you when your enemies will build an embankment against you and encircle you and hem you in on every side. They will dash you to the ground, you and the children within your walls. They will not leave one stone on another, because you did not recognize the time of God's coming to you."[107] Just thirty-seven years later, this would come about in the Roman's bloody capture of Jerusalem and the utter destruction of the Temple.

The crowd kept going before me and growing, for the people were telling others about the resurrection of Lazarus, and soon the whole city was in commotion, wanting to know, 'Who is this?' Seeing this, the Pharisees lamented, and they said, 'Look how the whole world has gone after him.'[108] Now it was an hour of glory, and although I knew it was on the surface only, provided to me as a gift from the spirit, I allowed the people to rejoice, and I rejoiced with them.

That day I went to the temple and taught, and people again brought those who had not been cured, and I made them whole. And young boys in the temple cried out, "Save, we pray, the Son of David."[109] At this the Pharisees became incensed and cried to me, asking if I heard what they were saying, and I reminded them that it was out of the mouths of babes that praise would come. "From the lips of children and infants you have ordained praise."[110]

After I had finished teaching, I looked around the entire temple, and then I called my disciples so that we might depart the city and return to Bethany.

The next morning we rose early and made our way back to the city. As we walked toward Jerusalem I felt hungry and I saw a fig tree that was heavy in leaf, as it would be when it was ripe, and I walked to the tree, but it had no fruit. Spirit moved within me, and I grew angry, and said to the tree, "Let no one eat fruit from you anymore, forever."[111] I knew I was under strain, but I was a little surprised at this outburst, as were my disciples, and for a moment I was worried I had made an error, but spirit soothed us, so we kept going without a thought.

When we reached the temple I wanted to take care of something I had noticed the day before, so walking to the tables of the money changers and vendors, I proceeded to overturn their tables, and I drove them out, saying, "Is it not written, 'My house will be called a house of prayer for all the nations?' but you have made it a den of thieves."[112] For they were using the needs of the people to cheat them.

I spoke plainly that day, saying, "The hour has come for the son of man to be glorified, for I tell you truthfully, unless a grain of wheat falls to the ground and dies, it remains just one grain, but if it dies it bears fruit."[113] I talked to the people about the importance of not putting too much stock in this life, and tried to explain to them that the man with pure vision was not happy with the things of this world, but that he would be overjoyed with the things of the New One, and that if he would believe in me he would see this New World, although there would be hardship involved in following me. I became weighed down with the pressures that were coming in upon me, for I knew that the people did not really understand my words, and I could feel the presence of the dark spirit beginning to press upon me, for It knew, now, that I would not resist, and taking that as weakness, It began to gather in strength, becoming palpable. I was talking out loud, and I continued, "Now my soul is troubled, and what shall I say? 'Father, save me out of this hour?' No, it was for this reason I came to this hour,"[114] and I cried out, but humbly, "Father, glorify your name."[115] And I put away my concerns in submission, as one does in meditation. As I paused to let the self-correction I had made sink in, a great voice came from above, "I both glorified It, and I will glorify It again."[116] And it was the Voice of God.

The people were amazed, and afraid about what might happen, but I said to them, "This voice has occurred not for my sake, but for your sakes. Now there is a judging of this world, now the ruler of this world will be cast out."[117] After that the spirit of evil backed away from me for a time, but it went into the crowd, and they immediately said, "We heard from the law that the Christ remains forever. How is it you say that the son of man must be lifted up, who is this 'Son of Man'?"[118]

We continued teaching but it was the same. At twilight we again departed for Bethany, to the home of Martha and Mary and Lazarus, where we were staying.

It was now Tuesday morning and we again began our walk to the temple. We came to the fig tree that had drawn my anger the day before, and it was withered, without a single leaf, and dead. The disciples immediately pointed it out to me and I answered them, but in my mind spirit spoke to me, and told me why It had invoked my curse, for the fig tree was the Nation of Israel, and where it should have born fruit it did not, and the withering of the tree was a prophecy, that the Nation would not survive, because it had failed to recognize me, bringing pain to God, and to the world.

I knew that this would be the last day I would spend at the temple. But I felt strong. I looked to the horizon and beyond so that I could feel the full expanse of spirit, and I thought about what I would say and do on this day. I tried to think if I had left anything out, if there was something I could do to help my disciples or anyone that might be on the verge of understanding. I really could not think of anything, so I decided to limit what I said to prophecy draped in allegory, knowing it would be available to those later on who would have a better perspective on things and be able to see more clearly what had happened and why.

Before I had even arrived at the temple the Pharisees were out to challenge me, but I answered their question with a more difficult one, and when they could not answer, I refused to answer them. Perhaps it was a small human satisfaction I allowed myself. Later when their nagging had subsided, and we were at the temple, I told a story for the benefit of my followers, to show them that the Pharisees were not merely confused and well intentioned at heart, but that they were motivated by the same selfish forces that create such pain and suffering on this earth.

The story goes like this. A certain man planted a vineyard, and he worked hard to make it good. He built a fence around it, and dug a winepress, and erected a tower that would serve as a dwelling and a place of refuge. Since he was going away to a far land he rented

167

the vineyard out to a group of men who were to operate it and keep its produce, giving him only a small share each year. When the end of the first productive year came, the man dispatched a servant to go and see how things were going and to bring some of the wine as had been agreed. But when the servant arrived, the tenants took hold of him, and beat him, and when the man sent others they did the same; some they stoned and some they beat to death. Finally the man sent his own son, thinking that they would come to their senses and make amends, but the men, knowing this was the heir to the vineyard, killed him as well, hoping to make the vineyard their own.

At this point I asked the religious leaders around me in the temple, "What, now, will the owner of the vineyard do?" They answered easily, "Because they are evil, he will bring an evil destruction upon them and will let out the vineyard to other cultivators, who will render him the fruits when they become due."[119] By their own words they condemned themselves. And I gave further warnings from scripture, and when the Pharisees realized that it was to them I was referring, they surged forward to kill me, but they decided better of it, for the large crowd knew I was a prophet, and it would have been difficult to take me.

I was not yet through, so I told another illustration, and I said that the Kingdom of Heaven had become like a king who prepared a great marriage feast for his son. The king sent his servant out to call all those who were invited, but for one reason or another they refused to come. The king sent servants out again, all saying 'Look, the food is prepared and the tables are set,' but again they would not come, some going to their own fields to work and some to their businesses, but the rest mistreated his servants and killed many of them. At this the king grew angry and sent his armies, and he destroyed the men and burned their cities. And then the king told his servants that since the feast was prepared, to go to the roads outside the city and ask anyone they met to come to the feast. When the feast was underway the king came in to see how things were going, and when he saw a man who was not wearing a marriage garment, he asked the man how he had gotten in without a marriage garment. The man was speechless and the king had him thrown out. "For many are called, but few are chosen,"[120] I ended. I realized that this story was not for those around me listening, but was for the future. The first servant represents my ministry, and the second group of servants stands for the time to come when my disciples would receive my holy spirit after I had ascended, and go out to preach to Israel for a time equal to my Work, both attempts failing to bring Israel to the status of accepting what God had offered. But I will tell you now that the man who is discovered without a marriage garment represents christians throughout history, and today, who think that they understand, but do not, and who, despite their sense of believing they are invited, do not have the approval of God because they do not do the things that are truly in harmony with Truth, and they do not seek the Truth with sincerity and humility and with kindness, as is required. If they had looked they would have seen that the servants were making wedding robes available to all who came, because the king knew many of them were poor, even in spirit. What was needed would have been provided if they had but asked. But because of the ease with which the invitation came, they were smug, and felt their lack of respect would be of no consequence.

Even as I was saying these things the Pharisees and the high priests, along with the officers of Herod, were trying to find a way to capture me without arousing the crowd. They sent a group of shrewd men to try and corner me by their questions, so they could raise doubt in the crowd, and take the opportunity to seize me. One of the questions concerned the resurrection, and they gave me an analogy that went like this. There was a man, who was happily married, but he died, and his brother married his wife. In our tradition if a man dies it is considered good if the man's brother marries the widow, for he will be likely to take good care of her and raise her children with love. The story continues; as it turned out the second brother died, and then the third, and so on, until the woman ended up being married to all seven brothers. So they asked me, 'In the resurrection which man will be the woman's husband?'[121] I looked at them and merely shook my head, and I said to them, "Is not this why you are so stupid, not knowing either the scriptures or the Power of God? For when they rise from the dead, neither do men marry nor are women given in marriage, but are as angels in the heavens."[122] This was said to answer them and to confuse them, but since it has confused so many people from that time on, leading many to think that this meant there would be no gender in the New World, I will explain some of it to you now, as it is known by the wise. When man is resurrected it will be to the New World of God. This world will be without Satan or the influence of evil of any kind, and it will have the Glory of the Light of God and of the Son of God, and the full help of God's Spirit. When a creature is in harmony with the Spirit of God he is lead by that Spirit, just as I was when I lived upon the earth. When a man is lead by Spirit he is free (as the scriptures tell us at 2Corinthians 3:17, since I am speaking to you today) and when man is in harmony with God there is no need of marriage or other law that governs the actions of men, for men will know the law, and it will be in their hearts, just as it is with the angels.

"What is the greatest commandment in the law?"[123] They asked me next, and I gave them my words, which are well known on the earth, but largely ignored. "Love the lord God with all your heart, and with all your soul and with all your mind, this is the first and greatest commandment, and the second is like it. Love your neighbor as yourself."[124] For if we did these things God would not have had to create the law, or send the prophets.

It was a long day, and this sort of thing went on until the late afternoon, for I continued to denounce them as hypocrites and liars, which they were, and it is the same today, for the leaders of men are liars and hypocrites, and the people are mislead, just as they were.

Many of the crowd listened with pleasure, but not the Pharisees, and at the end I was distressed. I said out loud how I had wanted to bring comfort to the people, but they would not have it, and so I said to all Jerusalem, "Look! Your house is abandoned to you."[125]

The disciples and I made our way out of Jerusalem for the last time.

As we passed the temple the disciples were marveling over the great temple walls, which were indeed impressive, in places each stone was some thirty-five feet long and fifteen feet thick and ten feet high. I suppose after such a difficult day even the strongest of them was shaky, and they welcomed the thought of something as solid and secure as the sight of these great stones laid, it seemed endlessly, one upon the other, with design and purpose. I felt their need, but I was not going to deceive them. I knew that what they really wanted they would have to look for elsewhere, so I said to them, "Do you behold these great buildings, and these great walls, by no means will a stone be left here upon a stone and not be thrown down."[126] I know that this seemed a bit oppressive to them, but it was not I who made it so.

They were quiet for a while, thinking about what I said and wondering what it was really all about, and I issued spirit to them to help them contain the matter. When we came to the eastern slope of the Mount of Olives, we sat down to rest and look out over the city and the great temple. It was a beautiful place, warm with the spring, and the gentle trees bright with new growth, and the color of the new flowers giving soft diversion to the eye, so I went off a little way to sit, and breathe the sweet smelling air, and relax.

A few minutes had passed, and it seemed we had all regained our strength, for Peter and James and Andrew and John came over to me; they had obviously been thinking about what I had said concerning the temple, and they were trying to fit it all in.

They had been thinking about my prophecy regarding the destruction of the temple, and about my sayings that talked about the end of the world and my return to it as King, and they wanted to know specifically what I meant. I sensed they had accepted that I was leaving them, and they wanted this question, which remained a mystery, answered plainly before I left. So John asked me directly, obviously having composed the question between them, "Tell us, when will this happen, and what will be the sign of your coming, and of the end of the world?"[127]

When I began to answer the question I felt the spirit become active, and I knew that the answer would be long and not easy to unravel. The important thing to me about their question was that at least they had come to terms with some things. Firstly, they knew that I was leaving them, and secondly, they knew I was coming back, and that when I arrived it would signal the conclusion of the Age, or what we call the end of the world.

I thought it a very good question, and I considered it for a while before I answered. Judgment day was not a new concept to our people. It was present in the Prophets, and with Moses and in the Psalms. Much of that prophecy was warning about specific events that would come upon Israel as a result of their forgetting about God and what He meant, and as a result of them becoming the type of people that God could not protect; cruel and violent and without justice, no different from the nations of the world. Those things had already occurred by the time of my life, but woven into those ancient prophecies were also warnings about what was to happen in times that had not yet come.

While I was thinking, the other disciples came over and I began to answer the question. I didn't have too much time left and what I had to say needed to be said, so it was a long answer, intended for scripture as much as for my disciples. Later on I spoke to the four by themselves, going over some of the things I said in more detail, so they would have a more specific answer to what they wanted to know.

The next day we remained in Bethany and did not go to the temple. When I was alone with the four, I told them truthfully, again, that no one knows the exact time of the end of the world, or the end of the present system, as we more precisely put it in our own language, but God Himself. But I would tell them this, there were two things they had asked me, and my prophetic answer as it was recorded covered both things, one a small fulfillment and the other the large, as it often is with prophecy, just as Solomon foreshadowed my own future reign, and both events are covered by much of the same prophesy, with the prophecy concerning my reign as the son of David clearly extending beyond those that applied to Solomon, and applying to a rulership that would include all the nations of the world and be without death and without disease and without limitations in time. I told them plainly that the destruction of Jerusalem and the so-called end of the world were similar in prophecy to those about Solomon and Myself. Much of the language applied to both the end of the Jewish world as a nation of God for their denial of the One sent to them, culminating with the total destruction of the temple; and much of it to the end of this world as a whole, as the dark, violent, and spiritually disconnected world that is the only world man has ever known, a world doomed whatever had occurred with Israel. Both prophecies were wrapped in the same words, but some of those words applied beyond the destruction of the Jewish system and referred to the final events that signaled the end of the world as we know it, and the beginning of a new world, unlike what we even imagine. But I told them to be of good heart, for although they would be persecuted just like their teacher, they would endure, and that I would bring them to me in the world of God, and beyond that I would say no more, but it was enough.

Even I could not tell them exactly what the future held, for, as I mentioned before, I had not yet accomplished what was the most important reason for my life. I felt certain in my own heart that it would be done, but I was too wise to consider it already finished, even as close as I was, remembering a phrase still familiar to men, 'There is many a slip between the cup and the lip.'

In the answer I gave to my disciples that day on the Mount of Olives, spirit said many things that were meant for the people who will read this story, and I wonder that they are not better known, at least the plain things. Because their question clearly asked about my coming again to the earth, and the end, and when it might be, and it is fair for man to consider such things.

"For nation will rise against nation and kingdom against kingdom, and there will be food shortages and earthquakes in one place after another. All these things are a beginning of pangs of distress."[128] Man has always had such things, in all times, but despite that do not become so hardened that you cannot see. For if you cannot see you will miss what is obvious. "Now learn from the fig tree as an illustration on this point: Just as soon as its young branch grows tender and it puts forth leaves, you know that summer is near. Likewise also you, when you see all these things, know that he is near at the doors. Truly I say to you that this generation will by no means pass away until all these things occur."[129] Already they are being gathered together, and the two witnesses lie dead. And as for the nature of my coming, for those of you who think it may apply only to each man upon his death, "And this good news of the kingdom will be preached in all the inhabited earth for a witness to all the nations; and then the end will come."[130] Is that not specific enough? When I say, "When the Son of man arrives in his glory, and all the angels with him, then he will sit down on his glorious throne. And all the nations will be gathered before him…"[131] are not the words angels and nations enough to show that this event concerns both heaven and earth, even when they are repeated again, "And then the sign of the Son of man will appear in heaven, and then all the tribes of the earth will beat themselves in lamentation, and they will see the Son of man coming on the clouds of heaven with power and great glory"[132]

It was Wednesday morning. On Thursday afternoon my disciples and I would leave our hosts and travel to Jerusalem for the Passover dinner. Until then I wanted to do nothing. At the house of Martha and Mary and Lazarus I was very much at home, even more than at Capernaum with my disciples, although I loved that place and all it had offered me. But here it was almost as if I was once again in Nazareth, before the weight of knowledge had called me from that house and from that life. I dislike using the words knowledge and weight in the same breath, but it is true they come together, though it should never be a discouragement, because the strength and joy that come from Truth make the weight little more than a feeling of purpose.

But on this day I wanted as little of the weight as I could manage, and my friends made it so that I could scarcely keep my feet on the ground. There was no doubt that Martha made me feel happy, and on that day she made a point to be with me, and for the first time since I had known her she left the preparations to the others, I think just to show me that she remembered the advice I had given her some months before, about being so busy looking after others that she forgot to enjoy herself.

The day went slowly, with lots of time for simple talk, and a chance for some of the twelve to single me out, and ask me about something that was bothering them, or some concern for the future, and I was able to say to each one privately how much I cared for him and how proud I was of him. Judas was withdrawn and said little, for he did not think I knew about his intentions. After midday he made an excuse to go, saying he had things to do regarding our belongings, but he went off to Jerusalem, and there he made an agreement with Caiaphas, who was meeting with the elders and the chief priests, to betray me; agreeing to lead them to me at a moment when I would be away from the crowds, and easy to seize.

We had a beautiful meal, and Mary once again rubbed the fine nard into my feet, and into my hair, for she had saved a portion from the feast at Simon's house. Although I know she would have used it all that evening, simply to prickle her critics, when I had defended her she had saved enough for tonight, and it was this oil that was to be the final dressing for my burial, which I had alluded to, with double meaning, the other night. The scent of the fine oil that Mary had applied to me filled the room in such a beautiful way that I knew spirit had augmented it, perhaps as a sign of just how wonderful things were to be one day upon the earth.

At the end of the evening I took Martha aside and I put my arms around her. As I was hugging her the pressure of her flesh seemed to melt away and it was as if my body was falling and falling into a void without end. There was absolutely nothing carnal about our embrace, Martha was as well versed in the law as I was, and we had both long since dealt with any spark of desire that may have arisen to tempt us, but I loved her very deeply. She represented the completion of my limited relationships with women, in a romantic way, on the earth. I kissed her cheek and we retired to our rooms. The next morning she did not appear, and I would never see her again while I was alive.

# CHAPTER ELEVEN

We left for Jerusalem late the next morning, and we took our time. We stopped on the Mount of Olives and I sent John and Peter into the city to prepare the room where we would have the Passover meal. I had arranged the place in secret, because I knew Judas had betrayed me, and I did not want our last meal together to be disturbed by those that sought to capture me.

The ten and I remained on the mountain, overlooking the sunlit city, and the temple. We did not speak a great deal, and when evening was approaching, we got up and made our way to the place I had arranged.

We climbed the stairs to the large upper room where we were to eat, and it was ready. With the help of our host, Peter and John had made the room everything I could have asked for. It was sparse, but the table and the furnishings were good, and the result was a comfortable and kind ambiance, filled with light and a certain majesty. After we had reclined for the meal a small silence came over us as our eyes surveyed the table and then came together over it. "I have greatly desired to eat this Passover with you before I suffer," [133] I said. And with that wine was poured and we began to eat and drink.

As I accepted the third cup I passed it to John, saying, "Take this and pass it from one to the other among yourselves, for I tell you, from now on I will not drink again from the product of the vine until the Kingdom of God arrives." [134]

After I had given the disciples the sincere lesson regarding the importance of being humble and of really trying to help each other as men, I returned to my place. Although I was still amused by Peter's reaction to my washing their feet, I turned to another matter, and I quoted the scripture, "He that used to feed on my bread has lifted up his heel against me."[135] In the silence that followed I became upset, and I said, frankly, "One of you will betray me."[136] They also became troubled and one by one said, "It is not I, is it?"[137] Even Judas said this. Now as I dipped my bread into the common bowl I went on to say that it was indeed one of the twelve, and I explained that, although it was true that I must go away, it was a dire thing for the man who betrayed me. With that I turned to Judas and said, "What you are doing get done more quickly."[138] The other disciples did not know what I meant by that, thinking I had asked him to do one chore or another in preparation for the rest of the festival. But at that moment Satan took the opening in Judas' heart, and he rose, and went out into the night.

When he had gone I relaxed, and after a while I took a loaf of bread and said a prayer of thanks over it. I then broke off a piece for each one, and I told them to eat it, and I said, "This means my body which is to be given in your behalf. Keep doing this in remembrance of me."[139] When they had eaten I took the fourth cup of wine and said a prayer over it, and as I passed it to them, telling them to drink, I said; "This cup means the new covenant by virtue of my blood, which is to be poured out in your behalf."[140]

A little later a dispute arose between Peter and John and James as to who was the greatest among them, this being partly because of the wine and partly because I saw that they still had not got the message concerning the dangers of wanting to place one man above another. I stopped them and said to them, with all seriousness, that they should take a look at themselves and at the world, and the plight of men. Their Kings and rulers lord it over them even with the power of death, and even the petty men with authority make their lives miserable and still want to be called benefactors. I pointed out that, in fact, I was the greatest of them, but my life had been spent in nurturing them and that this is what ministering must mean to them; to absolutely not accept the idea that any man was of more value than any other, until that judgment was finally made by God. Until then it was their duty to try and make the other man more worthy than they. When this had sunk in I said to them, "I make a covenant with you, just as my father has made a covenant with me, for a kingdom, that you may eat and drink at my table in the kingdom, and sit on thrones to judge the twelve tribes of Israel."[141]

I have to make a comment here. I had known for some time that these men were gifts to me from my father, and as time went on I saw that because I loved them He was going to allow me to take them into heaven with me, and to be with me as spiritual creatures when I came again to the earth. But this did not mean that every man that dies and is good, goes to heaven. It is the earth that will realize the New World, just as it is said, "He who created the heavens, he is God; he who fashioned and made the earth, he founded it; he did not create it to be empty,"[142] In honesty, it is not that complicated, but the father of confusion has managed to make the issue so muddled in the thoughts of men that even when they think of me it is without accuracy.

After I had made this covenant with my disciples I also gave them a command. "I give you a new commandment, that you love one another; just as I have loved you, that you also love one another."[143] At the moment I was speaking, we were all judged under the Law of Moses, but as my death was to be the fulfillment of the Law of Moses, after I was gone this new commandment was to remain as the single one upon which hangs the sword of justice. I spoke to them about other things that night, repeating the promise that my Father would send the spirit to them as their helper, and I prayed to my Father in their presence, that He look after them, and we sang songs, as was our tradition.

It was getting late, and I could see they were still troubled, so I said to them, "I leave you peace, and I give you my peace…. Do not let your hearts be troubled."[144] And I explained, "If you loved me, you would rejoice that I am going my way to the Father, because the Father is greater than I am."[145] Shortly after that I felt the touch of blackness, and I said, "I shall not speak much with you any more, for the ruler of the world is coming. And he has no hold over me."[146] I sat, feeling the pressure of the night close around me, and I said, "Get up, let us go from here."[147]

We left the room and headed back toward Bethany. As we walked I continued to talk. I reminded them that I would send the spirit of God to them, and that spirit would bring back to them all the things I had said. I mentioned this again because when I had explained to them that the ones who loved me would observe my words, and for that the father would love them, they were all straining to remember the things I had said to them over the past years, and were having trouble recalling them. Now really they knew what I had said to them, for the commandment to love includes those things, but also to bear fruit, they had to know how to describe Me and who I was according to scripture, so that the seeds could be planted in men who had no knowledge of me or of who I was. The Word would become, 'This means everlasting life, the taking in knowledge of you, the only true God, and of the one whom you sent forth Jesus Christ.'[148] It is the knowledge contained in the Scripture that allows a man the spark that will ultimately clear away the web of illusion that is over the earth, disclosing the Truth.

It was after midnight and cool, but the night was oppressive. felt thin, and quick things seemed to tear the fabric of the dark an disappear. I felt the pressure of fear trying to find a hold upon me, but I would not let it. But some thoughts had a ring of truth, and I let them enter my mind so that I could think about them. My body felt sensitive, feeling the grasp of unfriendly hands. I knew I had to let go, I knew that I had to surrender to this course of action ahead of me, but it was that itself that made it difficult for me. If I could have called upon the spirit to defend me, or if I could have allowed it to work through me so that I could defend myself, I would have found strength in the power I would exert to protect myself, and as the universe had no judgement against me for error, I would have prevailed against any force that came upon me. But I was not able to do this, for I had agreed with the will of God that I accept however the world chose to deal with My Presence. The trouble was that since I could not rally the forces of truth in my defence, I suddenly found that I was weak; and the thought was pressing that the very act of allowing Myself to be overcome could leave the world with the impression that perhaps I was not who I claimed to be. After all, look at him now, where now is all his arrogance? These thoughts were strong, and I was filled with an icy chill that seemed to make it even more difficult to dispel them.

We came to the garden of Gethsemane, a place on the first slope of the Mount of Olives, where the twelve and I had often come to escape the throng and to talk and pray. Now I was nervous, for I did not want to be captured in the state of mind I was in, and I asked eight of the men to remain at the entrance to the garden, and I took John and Peter and James into the deeper parts, were we had often sat before. I confided in them, and said, 'My soul is deeply grieved, even to death,'[149] for I was almost too weak to walk, 'Stay here and keep on the watch with me.'[150] Moving a little away I dropped to the ground and began to pray, "My father, if it is possible, let this cup pass away from me,"[151] but even as I said it, I knew it came from fear, and I added, "Yet not as I will, but as You will."[152]

I realized that I was going to be impaled, a fact I had never given my full attention. To be impaled was the worst of deaths in terms of shame, for such a man had no pity from his fellow man, the judgement itself testifying that he had done something despicable, receiving the rightful fate of a blasphemer. The thought pounded at me that perhaps I had done something wrong, that to die in this fashion might in some way take away from the sanctity of God's Name, upon which I had relied and of which I had spoken so frequently. I continued to pray but found no answer, so I turned to John and Peter, for support, but I saw that they were in deep sleep. "Could you men not so much as watch one hour with me? Keep on the watch and pray continually, that you may not enter into temptation."[153] Even as I said the words I realized that the full power of the force of darkness was upon us, and that the only way their bodies and minds could survive was to become unconscious, so I said, almost to myself, 'The spirit, of course, is eager, but the flesh is weak.'[154] I went a further distance away and I prayed again, feeling something must be out of order, but I could determine nothing, and again when I returned the three were asleep. With some resignation I roused them, but they could say nothing. A third time I retired to prayer, and on my knees I asked again that this type of death not occur, to die as a man who curses God simply did not seem right, how could this bring glory to my Father. As I was praying an angel came over me and spoke to me, "What you are feeling and thinking is from the evil one, for he has taken you," he said, "You are doing as you should, do not be afraid." With these words I caught a sense of what was going on, that since I was unable to defend myself from the spirit and mind of Satan, he had actually been able to shape what I thought and did, and I was relieved that the thoughts were not my own. I continued on my knees and simply let the black force be within me, doing and saying what it would, but now I simply stood aside, helpless but separate. I could feel the storm of thought rage through my body screaming its sharpened half-truths and searching for my own concession to their truth. But I was secure now, although the sheer force of the malignant spirit wracked my body, and blood seeped through my skin, wrung from my body by the emotions that my nervous system could not contain.

I pulled myself up and walked back to where Peter and James and John were again huddled in sleep, and I said to them, 'At such a time as this you are sleeping and taking your rest?'[155] But I said it with a note of humor, for I had regained myself. So I said to them, "It is enough. The hour has come. The Son of Man is betrayed into the hands of sinners. Get up, let us go. Look, my betrayer has drawn near."[156] I saw the lights of torches and heard the clamour of a mob.

The three and I joined the others at the entrance to the garden, and we now watched as the crowd of men approached. It was a large group, made up of soldiers, Pharisees, and a few common people who had followed along behind. It was dark and I saw that the soldiers did not recognize me, but were looking from one man to the next. Judas then approached me, and saying, "Good day, Rabbi,"[157] he kissed me on the cheek. "Fellow, for what purpose are you present?"[158] I asked him, and then said, "Judas, do you betray the Son of Man with a kiss?"[159] I knew that the kiss was the way Judas had arranged to identify me to the soldiers. I then stepped past him and into the light of the torches. "Who are you looking for?"[160] I asked, and the commander of the guards said, "Jesus the Nazarene." "I am he,"[161] I said, taking another step forward. As I stepped further into the light, spirit brightened my image, and the men moved back, many of them falling to the ground.

"I told you I am he,"[162] I said, tired of the game. "If therefore it is I you are looking for, let these go."[163] I wanted to indicate to the disciples that they need not be bound with me, and I also wanted the soldiers to be discouraged from capturing them as well, while I still had some authority. The soldiers regained their composure and came to me and began to bind my wrists. As they did this Peter seemed to suddenly realize what was going to happen and he called to me, "Lord, shall we strike with the sword?"[164] and as was Peter's way, he acted before I could speak, and taking one of the swords we had with us he moved to the crowd and struck off the ear of a man in the front of the group of officials. Now some have said that Peter missed the man, only to strike the ear, but that was not the case, for Peter was skilled, and he cut the man's ear off as an attempt to make the men withdraw. I did not want my men killed, so I stopped him, and I loosed the bonds that were around my wrist and lifted the man's ear up to his head, and healed him. After correcting Peter I explained to my disciples, and for the sake of the Pharisees, "How would the scriptures be fulfilled that it must take place this way?[165] The cup that my father has given me, should I not drink it?" [166]

I then turned directly to the crowd and asked them, "Have you come out with swords and clubs as against a robber, to arrest me? Day after day I used to sit in the temple teaching, and yet you did not take me into custody. But all this has taken place for the scriptures of the prophets to be fulfilled."[167] At this the commander of the soldiers and several of his men advanced upon me and bound me. The disciples were pushed back, and they began to flee. However in the crowd was a young man, a follower of mine named Mark, and Judas recognized him and the soldiers attempted to seize him, but he pulled out of his linen tunic, and escaped.

I was taken to the home of the influential former high priest Annas. Annas had been the high priest when I had attended the temple as a boy, and after the allotted time his sons also had become the high priest, and at the present time the name of the High Priest was Caiaphas, who was Annas' son-in-law. Because of all this Annas was a powerful man in the Land of Israel. The soldiers had brought me to him as they had been ordered, in order that his son-in-law

Caiaphas might have time to bring together the Sanhedrin, the holy court of the land. Annas began to question me about my teaching and about my disciples, but I said, "I have spoken to the world publicly. I always taught in a synagogue and the temple, where all the Jews come together; and I spoke nothing in secret. Why do you question me? Question those who have heard what I spoke to them. See. These know what I said,"[168] indicating the Pharisees and the soldiers present. At this a soldier standing near me struck me in the face, saying, 'Is that the way you address the chief priest?' "If I spoke wrongly," I replied, "bear witness concerning the wrong. But if rightly, why do you hit me?"[169] At this I was lead away, still bound, to Caiaphas.

The Sanhedrin is composed of 71 men, and yet the front room of the high priest Caiaphas could contain them all in comfort. Soon they were all present, but they had been delayed in finding witnesses against me. Such a trial, in the dark of the night on Passover, was not within the law, but they continued, because they had already decided to put me to death. I had become composed again, and, as I looked on, the room took on a sense of unreality, the harsh cruel countenance of the men holding little similarity to the image I, and my people in general, held of the great court.

After a long time two witnesses were brought forward. One began, "We heard him say, 'I will throw down this temple that was made with hands and in three days I will build another not made with hands.'"[170] Caiaphas asked me, "What is it these are testifying against you?"[171] But I remained silent, and the witnesses began to squabble with each other, not being able to make their stories agree. I watched Caiaphas as he walked away, disappointed, and then turned toward me, satisfied with his thoughts, "By the living God I put you under oath to tell us whether you are the Christ the Son of God!"[172] Although I rarely said such a thing directly, I had no intention of lying, and so I said, "I am; and you persons will see the Son of man sitting at the right hand of power and coming with the clouds of heaven."[173]

At this, Caiaphas, in a dramatic display, ripped his garments and exclaimed: "He has blasphemed! What further need do we have of witnesses? See! Now you have heard the blasphemy. What is your opinion?" "He is liable to death,"[174] the Sanhedrin proclaimed unanimously.

As I stood before them, my hands tied behind my back, they began to become bold, and they jeered at me and some began to strike me in the face. One priest pulled my tunic over my face and hit me with force, and called out, 'Prophesy to us, you Christ. Who is it that hit you?'[175] The blows that followed seemed as little to me, and I paid attention to keeping my balance, as I did not know from what direction the next strike would come, but this soon passed, and I was taken out from the house.

I had waited for an hour or so before the dawn came, and I was taken again to another place, which I recognized as the Hall of the Sanhedrin. Still clinging to some hope of respectability, the court had been called again, this time in the light of day and at the appropriate place. Now they started up again, and asked me, "Are you, therefore, the Son of God?"[176] And I simply replied, "You yourselves are saying that I am."[177] This was enough for them, and they reasoned that they needed no witnesses, having heard it from my own mouth. With this they led me out to the Roman Governor.

As we approached the palace of the governor it was still early morning, and there was no one about, being the day after the Passover meal. I had a strange combination of thoughts and feelings. I was resigned about the injury I had and would receive, and in some way I was not even interested in what was happening, merely impatient that things be over with. But as we approached the steps of the mansion I became more alert, and I oriented myself, for here I was before the great power of the world, Rome, to whom I had not even attempted to preach, and I was curious. The men of the Sanhedrin would not enter into the building, as it was considered unclean, and so, after a few minutes the consul came out to us, and he stood on the steps above us and asked what it was we wanted of him. He was not a young man, and I thought he looked older than he was, in some way, because his straight, once handsome features were somewhat puffed from the strain of office and the results of too much wine. But his eyes were intelligent, and confident in the wisdom that resided in them. He was very alive, and seemed to enjoy even the words that came out of his mouth, almost listening to them and reassessing them as he heard them with his own ears. I could see that he felt himself to be a part of Rome, much in the way a believer feels he is a part of his own God, and when he spoke he allowed the greater part of himself, the power and authority of Rome, to carry the words. He immediately confronted the piety of the Sanhedrin by asking them what accusation they brought against me, and he looked at me but I could determine nothing of his assessment. The court matched his disdain and answered that if I were not a wrongdoer they would not have brought me to him. I knew such an approach would not succeed with this man, and he turned to go, saying, "Take him yourselves and judge him according to your own law."[178] There ensued a general uproar, and he turned back to us and waited. A spokesman for the priests came closer, and he said, "It is not lawful for us to kill anyone,"[179] and as Pilate, for that was his name, hesitated, the spokesman for the group retired to the crowd and returned with a parchment. The Jews had decided not to mention their own trial, knowing that Pilate might do just as he had done, instruct them to deal out their own justice as it was a matter of religious legality, so they had written down a list of charges that had at least a thread of honesty connected to their complaint with me, and that they hoped would concern Rome. The spokesman now read out the charges, which were three. I was charged with: subverting the Nation of Israel, forbidding the paying of taxes to Caesar, and calling myself Christ, a King.

I could see that at least one of these charges caught his attention, but he turned and walked away without a word. We waited for what seemed a long time, although I suppose it was only five minutes or so. The priests were uncomfortable and began to squirm about, glaring at me and moving their feet, their minds busy with determination and rumination over why I was so despicable to them. Soon a guard came out and took me into the palace.

I walked up the steps and into a long marble hall, carefully but thinly adorned with well fashioned articles, a pair of torches each twenty paces, and a small table on each side of the corridor that held ledgers with the insignias of Rome. Alcoves held the busts of Caesars, past and present. At the end of the hall there were three columns on each side, and passing through them we came to a larger room, also marble but of a finer quality that gave off a luminescent coolness and a feeling of open grandeur. There were fine tapestries on the walls, and on the wall directly in front of me hung great banners bearing the powerful symbols of Rome. Almost in the middle of the room and facing the entrance was a chair, made of ivory and marble and adorned with little but a golden emblem in the center of the chair's back, just above the head of the man sitting there, watching as I approached. There was a table with the tools of writing on his left, a smooth slab of marble held by carefully wrought iron.

When I was still some twenty paces from him, he told me to stop and he looked at me. He looked to the side and then back toward me and asked, "Are you the king of the Jews?"[180] I wanted to know what he knew of me, and so I asked him, "Is this of your own originality that you say this, or did others tell you about me?"[181]

"I am not a Jew, am I?"[182] He said with sincerity, and I knew he knew nothing of me. "Your own nation and the chief priests delivered you up to me. What have you done?"[183]

"My kingdom is no part of this world,"[184] I told him, slowly and deliberately. "If my kingdom were part of this world, my attendants would have fought that I should not be delivered up to the Jews. But, as it is, my kingdom is not from this source."[185]

He considered this for exactly the amount of time it would take to understand such an answer, and then immediately asked. "Well, then, are you a king?"[186]

I said to him truthfully, "You yourself are saying that I am a king. For this I have been born, and for this I have come into the world, that I should bear witness to the Truth. Everyone that is on the side of the Truth listens to my voice."[187]

He paused for exactly one moment, then said, "What is truth?"[188] Without waiting for, or expecting, an answer, he rose from his chair and walked past me toward the entrance, gesturing to one of the soldiers to bring me with him. When we came out the Sanhedrin was standing as if they had not moved the whole time. He lifted his arm toward me and said; "I find no crime in this man."[189]

The Sanhedrin erupted in anger, and began calling out all at once, and, with a skill long perfected by the Jews, at some point their voice became one, saying, 'He stirs up the whole people, from Judea to Galilee.'[190]

When Pilate heard that I was a Galilean, he knew immediately what he would do, for Herod Antipas, the ruler of Galilee was in Jerusalem for the Passover. Pilate dispatched a soldier to Herod, and within a few minutes I was also on my way to the ruler.

Herod was a disheveled and unpleasant man, and I immediately saw that he had no interest in me, or the case against me, but hoped only to see a miracle, or a trick. I, myself, had nothing to say to this man, for I knew it was he that ordered the beheading of John the Baptist, and spirit did not urge me to talk. Herod was relived when he saw me, for he had heard about the miracles I was doing in Galilee, and had feared that I was John returned from the dead, with greater powers. This relief put him in a good mood, and seeing that my silence was adamant, he and his men made fun of me, but they did not harm me, and within the hour I found myself again in the anteroom of Pilate. Pilate called the Jews to him, who were milling around, waiting for an answer. When they had gathered, Pilate said to them, "You brought this man to me as one inciting the people to revolt, and, look! I examined him in front of you but found in this man no ground for the charges you are bringing against him. In fact, neither did Herod, for he sent him back to us; and, look! Nothing deserving of death has been committed by him. I will therefore chastise him and release him."[191]

I could see that Pilate was now under the impression that I was an innocent man, guilty only of the envy of the priests, and he wanted to release me. I myself was in an odd state of mind. I was not used to being dragged around from one place to another, and I too, wanted it to be over. I felt little; spirit was small within me, and I could feel no presence of the dark force. I could only wait.

And so it went. The Jews would not accept my release, and so Pilate proceeded with what he thought was a good idea. For the sake of the good will coming from such a gesture, the Romans had instituted a policy of releasing a prisoner, of the Jews choice, each Passover. So he called out a murderer from the prison, a man hated by the Jews, for he was guilty of many crimes against the people. And he offered the Jews the choice between us, which one would be freed. Now as this was taking place I began to lose interest in what was going on. I was tired, and I was having trouble concentrating. The priests spoke up loudly, and incited the crowd, which had grown as the day wore on, and they all cried out, "Barabbas," for that was the name of the murderer. As these things took place I began to fade into a stupor, for I could not stand to see the people so easily mislead. Among the crowd were many who had thrown palm leaves in my path as I had come into Jerusalem, and some of them I had even cured.

I was taken and flayed, and although I was numb I stood straight when I was commanded. After I was beaten I had little strength, but I relied on spirit, and for the dignity of my Father I remained tall and proud. I was taken before the people with a crown of thorns imbedded in my head, and with a purple robe cast over my shoulders, and still I was rejected, there being no pity among the crowd, as the Pharisees continued to shout out derision and many untrue things. I remember that I looked over to see Pilate washing his hands of me, and hearing the crowd scream, 'Yes, his blood upon us and our children.[192]' As I looked again to Pilate I saw in his eyes the beginning of awareness, the beginning of doubt in a world that for him had always been certain.

I was taken from the palace to the place of execution, and although I was ordered to carry the stake upon which I would be impaled, I had neither the strength nor the will to do it, and another was called upon to carry the pole. When we came to the place, it was a hill, unfamiliar to me in the state I was in. I was turned and pushed toward the spot where there were three poles lying on the ground, behind each pole was a deep hole. The soldiers came and drove a steel spike into each pole, about eight feet from the top of the pole, and after the spike was nailed in it was sharpened. An officer came to the pole that was in the middle, and near the top he nailed a sign that said: 'The King of the Jews', written in Hebrew and Latin and Coine. And this was my pole. I was taken and placed upon the spike, so that it pierced my intestines and came into my abdomen, and after that my hands were held above my head so that a great nail was driven into my wrists, and it passed through them into the pole. When this was complete I felt my legs being pulled together, and felt the pain of another nail, which was driven through my feet into the wood of the stake, so that my feet overlapped. Three men then came and took the pole and raised it upright and let it slide into the hole, and they shoveled rocks into the hole so that the stake would remain upright. I was only half awake as I watched the soldiers do these things, but I saw in their eyes no malice, only the practiced actions that come from long years of obedience and resignation and futility.

I remember very little of what happened next, except I know I opened my eyes at one point and I saw John standing with my mother. And I spoke to him, somehow, telling him that she was his mother now, to love and care for, and I saw in his eyes a smile, but it was soon covered by his own tears, and I looked away.

It came to be about the time of midday, and I was fading. The little strength I had left began to slip from both my body and my mind. With the failing of my consciousness the world began to appear dark, but I jerked awake for a moment when I noticed, with what little remaining awareness I had, a commotion in the throng. I could see from the actions and sounds of those gathered beneath me that the growing night was real to them as well. The withdrawal of my spiritual power was causing actual darkness on the face of the earth. Curiosity about this soon gave way to a deeper darkness. I was alone, without light, without knowledge, without time. I felt no spirit, no sense of God, and I heard myself cry out, "My God, my God, why have you forsaken me?"[193] I knew immediately after I had spoken these words that, indeed, all spiritual protection had been withdrawn from me, in order that I be tested to finality. Some thought that with these words I was crying out to Elijah, and they said, "See, he is calling Elijah."[194]

I felt coolness on my lips, and I instinctively drank. As the shock of the sour wine spread through my senses it carried a great wave of warmth and light, infused with a suffocating nausea. I knew it was over, and I spoke aloud in unison with the coming blackness that flowed behind the tide of sickness. "Father, into your hands I entrust my spirit."[195] I looked out ahead of me, and the horizon lay exactly in the middle of my field of vision, with a thin strip of blue running along it, but dark, to my eyes, below the line of the earth, and fading into gray and darkness above it. I closed my eyes and I felt a great shudder as the words came from my lips, and from above, in one utterance, "IT IS FINISHED."[196]

# CHAPTER TWELVE

The next thing I remember was that I opened my eyes. I saw only darkness, and as I looked into that darkness I saw light, a faint quiver of light. As I focused on it, it grew, into a point of brightness, and then quickly, instantly the cave was filled with the light of a dull morning. I hesitated, and then reached out within me to feel my body, and it was there. I felt a warm happiness within my stomach, and it flashed out, filling my heart and head, and my arms and my hands, and my hips and legs and even my feet. I lay silent for a moment, and then I sat up, my mind racing ahead of me, knowing that it was over. I was free again, I was I. I stood up, and behind me, with a faint brush of feeling, fell cotton strips wound in the shape of a body. My hands instinctively went to my head, and I felt a wrap of linen, which I removed and rolled into a coil, laying it at the head of the cotton body. I glanced toward what I knew was the entrance of the cave, and as I did, the great boulder that closed the tomb silently shifted so that the light of day came in. I stood still, and closed my eyes, gathering my thoughts. So it was over. I couldn't quite accept the full meaning of that. I walked to the entrance of the cave and went out. The day was shining. I looked at the trees, in bloom around the garden, and they became part of me, a part of creation I was familiar with. I looked to the sky and my eyes exploded upward, faster and faster, until the blue and brilliant light came to a great fullness, and the speed of my sight slowed, and turned with a slow and familiar curve into the great infinity of space, and then with a blink I was looking at the garden once again. I looked to the horizon and saw the white squares of buildings and the hint of motion that I knew was people moving in the streets. I clenched my fists and took a breath, then closed my eyes in happiness, for I had breath. I was alive. But for a moment I was puzzled, did I really still have a body? I looked down upon myself and, indeed, I saw a body; skin and feeling, a gash still upon my side that gaped open but felt whole, dried blood and open wounds on both my hands and feet, but no feelings of pain, or concern, on the contrary my body buzzed with energy and strength and certainty.

Not unlike when I had come out of the wilderness, fresh with enlightenment, I began to experiment, to see just what I was, for they were human memories flooding back into my mind. I remembered it all, as the images came before me, my mother, John, and John, and Peter, and Martha, and the Pharisees, and all the talk, and the closing in of darkness. I stopped there, and my mind obeyed instantly. I sank deeper into my mind, and thought about the thought of God. As I did this the light of the day came within me and I was filled with the great impulse of creation, the great brightness that holds all the sound and passion and feeling of life. I noticed my body fading into the light, and yet my human form held, but without wound or wrinkle; then it gave way to a finer form, still recognizable as the projection of myself, but hardly to be called physical. I maintained a conscious motion toward light, my body lifting up a few inches from the ground as I caught the feeling of it. I accelerated to the point I desired, and there I was, clouds wisping by my face, their moisture tangible and pleasant, and I turned to look, downward, toward the earth. I saw the city and I saw the temple, still a jewel from any angle, and I paused for a moment to collect my thoughts. I was alive. My father had given me life again, and I remembered that this was as it had been promised. So I must have succeeded! Joy punched out at me from within and I tried to remember just what it was I had succeeded at.

The great broad universe of thought surrounded me, and for the first time since my awakening I remembered it all. My heart and mind filled with the faces and names and feelings of everything I had experienced on the earth, although it was confined almost entirely to the time since my baptism. I looked again to the earth. I felt an anger toward those who had grasped this world from the great open heart of the universe, those who had brought such anguish, convincing man through force and cunning that the earth was a small and miserable place, by nature filled with pain and weakness. The anger grew and I pulled my right arm up beside my head, with my hand in a fist, as if to throw a throw a heavy javelin of thought into the heart of the planet, but I restrained myself, the great weight and energy my arm now held relaxing back into the endless sphere of the moment. And I lowered my head. No. It was the same.

But I was alive, and definitely with a new perspective. I was drifting above the city. I lowered my head and closed my eyes in prayer. Father. There was quiet darkness under my lids. I sent up thanks, and gratitude, for His wisdom and help. In the peace of the depths, I began to assemble all that had happened, and to look ahead. I opened my eyes and saw the great turmoil of the black spirit confined to the center of the earth. I saw the serpents' heads rising up to me from the earth in their spirit, calling out to me. With desperate taunts, "Are you going to kill us, Great One of God", they called, and I met their calls without thinking, "Don't look to me for comfort evil ones," I found myself saying. "Turn around and purify the world, and perhaps God will have pity on you." But they recoiled at my words, and for the moment I spoke no more to them.

Now this had broken the mood, and I began to move across the sky, finding it familiar and simple. My mind was clear. For me the end had become the beginning, but for the earth it was not so. I was alive, and I was still a man, I had every right to exercise my will as I chose. I was guilty of nothing, and my obligation to be passive, as had been the will of God, was gone. I heard murmuring below and anger returned. I sent a great blast of force to the earth, commanding the demons to be silent, and I warned them that whichever one of them raised its head to me again would have to test its full strength against mine. And they were quiet. And though I saw them creeping into the soil and the tiny microbes of the earth, I was content. It would be dealt with. One thing stood out in my mind like a pit before the steps of sanctuary, the Time of the Nations must run its course. This is the Time I spoke of previously, the time when the captive earth must remain burdened with the direction of Satan, and the other angels who had followed him to the earth, until it was evident to the great sword of universal justice that no future was possible for the planet on its present course. I thought that time must surely be close, but even as I said that to myself, I knew that this thing would be done with exactitude, known only to God and his Own Standards. So I was content with the retreat of the demons, and I made my way back to the surface of the planet to see the plight of my friends, to plant my feet on a strong rock, and to think and consult with spirit about what was to come.

I saw a mountain peak, far to the north of Judea and I headed for it. As I lit on the top, settling onto a rock that offered a comfortable surface, I felt my body resume its human form. I was a little puzzled by this, for after taking to the air I thought my human body was gone forever, at least gone from the solidity that it now took. As I looked down on my body I noticed that my wounds were not visible, but with the simple act of considering them, they came into view, and with a small amount of memory I was able to make them as visceral as I wished. I settled into the side of the stone with my right shoulder, and tucked my right leg up under my left thigh, my left arm settled across my stomach, and I felt at rest. My eyes surveyed the body. We had done a good job with this creation. The muscles and tendons of my limbs held the flesh in a smooth beauty, the natural position of my body lending repose to the strength of bone and muscle, giving off a slight glow of power. I snapped out of this admiration of myself, and pulled my body upright, summoning the mind and spirit together to think.

After I had entered into contemplation and the circle of my being stabilized to a warm, conscious light, I opened my eyes again, and I saw two white forms descending to where I sat. They were angels, but I didn't recognize them by name, and as is the way with us, their names came instantly to me, and I rose and greeted them. The one who was to speak said to me, "You have done well Michael," calling me by one of the names I held before my earthly life. "All things were accomplished. Would you like to see?" I answered yes, hearing my voice for the first time, and my mind became filled with vision. I saw myself upon the stake, and heard myself utter 'It is accomplished' in unison with a voice from heaven. This happened, I now observed, some three hours after normal daylight had ceased upon the earth, although I remembered no such length of time. I saw that much of celestial creation had gathered in the vicinity of the earth, arranged in random harmony that extended out beyond the galaxy, the spiritual and physical overlapping in space and time. At the moment of my death all external light had been withdrawn from the earth, darkness beyond the already unnatural night that held the earth and no light came from the temporarily isolated spirit creatures that ruled the planet. The voice of God spoke from heaven, and the vision showed that on the earth it was felt only as a great rumble. The voice said, "The earth is free from the bonds of sin, let every man decide to live or die without the fear of the judgment I once laid upon the sons of men. I have given the earth to my Son, and it is He who will dispense all further justice, and He who rules both life and death, in my Name and with my Spirit." As the voice subsided, all heaven erupted in jubilation, and praise was given God for his dealings with the earth, and to me for carrying out his secret plan. There was a great relief in the entire universe, for the pain of the earth had been felt by all creatures, and they had worried that the earth might simply spiral down to desolation. I noticed in the vision that I was not present, and remembered, of course, that at that moment I was without life, in emptiness with the dead of men, for the allotted time. But they did well without me, for the happiness extended in great brilliance, and continues. The light was released again upon the earth; the World had been judged. Satan would be allowed to run his course, but at the choice and will of God, to establish once and for all the futility and inevitable harm that comes from confronting the legitimacy of the center, the creator, to exert influence over the periphery, the creation. Satan had no further claim to man. My death had been the single most important moment in all the history of man, equal only to the moment that Adam had bitten the fruit. My life had allowed man the impossible, to choose life while he remained in death, to choose perfection from the state of ignorance, to transcend the reality of his existence as a flawed product of a doomed action. Man was free to answer in the present the question that had been asked and answered in the past, a simple question, Do you wish to live as a creation of God, accepting His will? A man will answer this question by accepting or rejecting the Life I was able to offer him through the authority I now possessed as the Living Cause of the universe, as it concerned the earth. I possessed this authority because I Had It. I was actually still a man but now more than a man. I was a man who was free of restriction, with the power to will whatever I chose, knowing from my heart and knowledge that it would be in harmony with the will of my Father. I had done what I had sacrificed my prehuman life to do. I had a new existence, as what I Was now.

As the vision faded, I met the angel's eyes with pleasure. I saw he had something to say, so I remained quiet and he spoke. "Officially all this has not been sealed until you appear before your Father. But He has given you forty days upon the earth to do as you please, and then we will return to take you Home." As he said this their wings raised up and extended out at the level of their shoulders, and they began to move off, and up, offering me their personal congratulations as they went.

I gave myself the pleasure of lowering my head, and allowing the full satisfaction of the moment to fill my being.

After a while, I myself took off, enjoying the feeling of flight without the nagging presence of the awareness that I had a body waiting somewhere to return to. I was truly myself again, whole and happy and free.

And I was still a man. That was the miracle of it all. I knew it was true that I was more than a man, but the human part of me remained intact and actual, my Father had resurrected me, not transformed me. And—the anticipation of it bursting out again—I saw that I could offer this same transformation to men, now being free to exercise the full power of my will, death having no real hold over mankind by the decree of the New Judgment. I had already resurrected men in my limited life on the earth, and now those I chose to bring to life had no reason to die again. The only gloom that remained was the allotted time for the earth to fulfill its dark destiny. This thought weighed upon me, but I could only see to go ahead and do the best I could.

I returned near the tomb, where I found the entrance still open. I knew it was early Sunday morning and I could see no one about, so I looked from above along the path to where the eleven were staying, and I saw a small group of women running in that direction. I came down in front of them and allowed my body to relax into its physical form, and I said to them, "Good morning." Thinking this was as good as anything. I recognized Mary, the mother of James, and John's mother Salome, and Joanna, so I said to them, "Do not be afraid, but be off to the brothers, that they may go into Galilee, and there they will see me."[197]

Again I returned to the tomb, and I saw that Mary Magdalene was standing near, and there were angels there. She turned and saw me and she did not recognize me, so I again spoke, saying, "Mary!" And she ran to me and buried her head in my chest and put her arm around me very tightly. I could feel her small muscular frame pressing against me, and I had to smile at her intensity, but I said, "Do not hold on to me, for I have not yet returned to the Father. Go instead to my brothers and tell them, 'I am returning to my Father and your Father, to my God and your God.'"[198]

Over the next few days I appeared several times to my disciples, and of course they were ecstatic that things were as they were. It was evident that despite all the times I had told them what was to happen, they really did not expect it to be so.

I did many things over the forty days, some of it for my own pleasure, and much of it to solidify the faith and knowledge of the brothers. I did go to my mother, and she was at peace, at last. I also came to my own brothers for the sake of my mother, that they might believe. And of the other times I came to men it is written about me. I just want to add that when I saw Peter, he was the most delighted of them all. I asked him three times if he loved me, and I told him each time he answered me to feed my sheep. I did this because Peter was in great pain about having denied me three times on the night of my capture. He did not understand at the time, but later when he began to worry about this again, spirit reminded him of my three times asking to declare his love for me, and explained that the three affirmations were for him to know he was forgiven, and not in debt.

The last time I saw the eleven it was near the Mount of Olives. I explained to them that the time of restoring the Kingdom of God to the earth was not up to us, but God, and then, after again promising them that I would send the Holy Spirit to help them, I felt a gentle tug. Responding, I began to drift higher into the air. As I looked down I saw the two angels that had come to me on the mountain speaking to the men, and then the disciples passed from my view, as the clouds closed around me. I looked up toward the heavens, and as I began to move more quickly the blue of the sky began to give way to the deep black of space. I was enjoying this sight when the two angels appeared beside me, and said to me, "We have been sent to bring you to your Father." With that our travel changed to light, and then to the great speed of the higher creatures of God, beyond time and space so that only the flicker of great celestial worlds was seen, with the gentle music they make blending into a fine hum, as we moved across the universe.

The Throne of God changes in appearance according to His will, although it is eternally in place, even when the Presence of God does not sit upon the throne. Whether God is there or not, there are always thousands of spiritual creatures around the throne, either doing the will of God or simply congregating and engaging the others that are there. The sacred area around the throne extends for a distance equal to all the universe perceived by man, and yet, such are the properties of this place, a spirit creature can see beyond the perimeter of the sacred area and view the great stars and celestial worlds that lie closest to the throne and past into the fading infinity of populated space beyond. This was not unfamiliar to me, naturally, having once lived here longer than any of the creatures present, but the wonder of the place does not diminish with time, and not having been here since my fall, except in the pure thought of spirit, it was humbling for me to see it all again. As we entered the area a great white pathway appeared in front of us. It became rather like a hallway of light, translucent, with an arched roof, so that we actually entered into it. I knew that this corridor was the welcome that accompanied a formal moment in the Court of the Living God. When we arrived at the end of the corridor, we entered through a highly ornate arch, which opened onto the inner court of the High God. On the level we were on there were massive columns that extended around the entire circle of this inner court. The columns surrounded a circumference so vast that on the opposite side of the throne, which appeared to be in the center of this space, they appeared as only a thin strip of gold light. I had never seen this before, and I think its purpose was to give the area of the throne the appearance of having spatial limitations, rather like the world I had just come from. It was in fact, humor, but I had been a man too long to catch it.

What was important was that I was to appear before God. I cannot describe much more to you, because it would begin to seem merely silly, but I hope that every man one day is able to come before God. It was a formal ceremony, as I said, and as I kneeled before God, He gave me praise for the Work that I had done, and although what I had done seemed as nothing while I knelt before Him, He denied that to the millions that watched, and He called me as His firstborn son, and a robe of finely woven light the color of blue and maroon together, was given me, and I sat down at his right hand on a great throne, and a crown of golden stars was place upon my head, and I was called the King of Heaven and Earth, in His name. All the creatures of heaven acknowledged this with a bow and an instant of submission, focusing, for a moment, all the power and glory and love of the universe onto the center of my being. Only certain ones were not present, for Satan would not appear.

In the heavens we do not lord it over one another, and it was unlikely that I would be called upon in my capacity as the King of Heaven for a very long time, by the measure of time, for all the creatures of heaven obey the will of God and the promptings of the Spirit. I had before known prominence in the heavenly worlds, being called the Word, but the Honor of sitting at the right hand of God was more than even I had considered, for It was what It was, and my love and gratitude to my Father cannot be described in words.

After the acknowledgement of the court, a great angel of God came before me and handed me the scepter that went with my station. And he gave me formal authority over the Earth, as had been explained to me before I ascended. He gave me the word from The Living God, my Father, that the twelve would be multiplied by their own number, and then by a thousand, as His gift to me in men, that they might be given the immortality of spiritual life, and reign with me over the earth for the thousand years allotted to returning the earth to perfection.

I was excused, for spirit knew I had things to do according to the brief years of man, and acts that I wanted accomplished before I rested. In that instant a four-winged angel, a messenger of speed, approached me and took my hand, and we were again at the gates of the throne, and then in the vicinity of the earth. I saw through spirit that the eleven were gathered together in an upper room with many others, and I ordered spirit to go to them and fill them with power beyond a man, and It did so. And with that the disciples began to teach, with the authority to baptize in spirit.

I saw that in my absence the disciples had replaced the position of Judas with a man named Matthias. Spirit had allowed this, knowing that I had been given an expanded number of people as a gift from the Living God, so I was not concerned with disappointing Matthias regarding his resurrection to the heavens along with the disciples. Spirit had also informed me of another man, Saul, a Pharisee, and I examined the man, and it was he I chose to replace Judas, for he was a man of extraordinary courage and determination. I placed Saul, who I renamed Paul, in charge of all the spreading of the Good News of the Redemption of Man throughout the world, because I knew the disciples were tired, and they lacked the strength to do what I needed done. After this I retired to a station above the world and I watched.

I cannot say I was surprised by what happened, for I knew the great strength of the darkness on the earth. There came a time when only John remained alive, and he was a prisoner, and bound in chains. By this time the dark force had already begun to insinuate itself into the congregations of God throughout the land. I watched as good men were turned to evil either by the subtle temptations of the authority they had been given in the congregation or the simple temptations of the flesh, and I had to observe the skill of Satan at first creating confusion, then offering clarity at the price of deviation from my command to love.

Seeing this all taking place, and unable to stop it without breaching the will of God that this matter run its course, I went to John in vision and I had him write the final book of scripture, which was sealed from understanding until your day. As spirit and I gave the words to John, I found myself newly excited about the news and details of the great and New Jerusalem, for this also was a device from my father that I had neglected in clarity until the spirit brought the words concerning it to earthly form. Now this new city was to be the manifestation of my victory, if you will, although spiritually it has been called a bride, symbolizing the union of heaven and earth. When the time came to renew the world, it was New Jerusalem, a city of dazzling spiritual beauty created by the Will of God Itself that was to be home to the apostles and those I had chosen from the earth. It was Spiritual Jerusalem that would come upon the earth to be the center of the great power that would restore the earth to the original perfection of Eden. Within its great walls there was a place for me, and happiest of all, the Father had made a place for Himself, so that He would be present on the Earth itself, for a time. From Its gates all the Chosen would go forth into the world at will, for they were all human in essence, they and I, and we could reform our bodies as we needed or desired. This vision as it was given to John was a source of great joy for me, because it brought with it the great promise of universal harmony, and a noble ending to a long and tragic story.

At the death of John, the brotherhood began to crumble. It would take a century or more before the work of Satan was complete, but I knew the issue from the seed. The ones who were trained to nurture by their leadership began to separate themselves above the ones who needed them, and they interpreted scripture as commands that I had never given and placed my name to them, and God's. They shielded themselves with the scriptures and my name, but they were as far from me as were the Pharisees that took my life. John had contained all this in the final book, but it was injury to me nonetheless.

Now I am almost through, but one event occurred that is a part of this story.

After I saw the way it was to be, and John was dead, I returned to my Father and I sat next to him and we talked, and I rested, while the allotted time went by. Satan was growing disturbed, for he could see a limitation to the course he had taken, and he made his way to the Throne, and he taunted me, for all the things that he had done and I had not tried to prevent. When this happened I rose straight up from where I sat, and looking to my father for approval, although I already had it in formality, I advanced upon him. Those angels that had taken his side in this thing also rose, and instantly I had allies by my side, and a great battle began, and all my anger came up within me and I drove him out of Heaven, and there was no where he could flee that I was not upon him, and finally he came to the earth, and there I left him.[199] But I commanded all the angels that he might not leave the air of the earth, and I posted eyes to watch him.

Satan began to make great havoc on the earth, although he tried to control himself, for the earth was all he had left, but he could not. These things and many others were as prophesied by John, for after I banished Satan from Heaven what was to follow meant crisis for the Earth, and I wanted the wise to know what was to come, so that there would be hope. I would not return to Heaven until It was complete. My following Satan out of heaven is spoken of by John as the going forth of the first of the four horses... "A white horse; and the one seated upon it had a bow; and a crown was given him, and he went forth conquering and to complete his conquest."[200] The other three horses represent the consequences of Satan's confinement to the earth after my aggression, and these continue to occur during your time. What is to come is also written. I could not stop the suffering, except for those who approached me in spirit and in truth, and to those I gave aid. But I knew the time was close, so I drew the forces of heaven to where they could wait to answer the call, and I sent the spirit to awaken what wisdom it could upon the earth, and to slowly open the book of John, and I set about to wait for the final time.

My presence was upon the earth, and It is. The boundaries between the fallen earth and heaven were dissolved where they overlapped with my conscious will, although this freedom is difficult for most men to avail themselves of, as it exists only in the higher attributes of man until the final day brings such Truth to the physical world. But I freely give hearing to all who will listen, and great things will occur upon the Earth as We approach.

# BIBLIOGRAPHY

---— ❦ ---—

The sole reference used is The Holy Bible

\*\*\*\*\*\*\*\*\*\*\*\*\*\*\*\*\*\*\*\*\*\*\*\*\*\*\*\*\*\*\*\*\*\*\*\*\*\*\*\*\*

## <u>List of Cited Scriptures</u>

[1] Joh4:24

[2] Mt3:14

[3] Mt3:15

[4] Mt3:17

[5] Joh1:29,30

[6] Joh1:36

[7] Joh1:38

[8] Joh1:39

[9] Joh1:42

[10] Joh1:47

[11] Joh1:48

[12] Joh1:49

[13] Joh1:51

[14] Joh2:16

[15] Joh2:18

[16] Joh2:19

[17] Ex12:26,27

[18] Joh2:23

[19] Joh4:9

[20] Joh4:10

[21] Joh4:11,12

[22] Joh4:14

[23] Joh4:15,16

[24] Joh4:18

[25] Joh4:19

[26] Joh4:20

[27] Joh4:23,24

[28] Joh4:25,26

[29] Joh4:50

[30] Lu4:21

[31] Lu4:22

[32] Mr1:24

[33] Mr1:25

[34] Mr3:11

[35] Mt9:9

[36] Mt9:14

[37] Mt9:15

[38] Mt9:16,17

[39] Mt12:2

[40] Mt12:10

[41] Mt12:11

[42] Mt12:12

[43] Mt12:13

[44] Mt3:2

[45] Lu7:14

[46] Lu7:19

[47] Ge3:4

[48] Ge3:5

[49] Lu7:40

[50] Lu7:41-43

[51] Lu7:44-47

[52] Lu7:48

[53] Lu7:50

[54] Mt14:28

[55] Joh6:28,29

[56] Joh6:34

[57] Joh6:42

[58] Joh6:51

[59] Joh6:53

[60] Joh6:60

[61] Joh6:67

[62] Joh6:68,69

[63] Joh5:20,21

[64] Lu12:51-53

[65] Mt17:5

[66] Mr9:19

[67] Mr9:24

[68] Mt17:22,23

[69] Joh7:4

| | | |
|---|---|---|
| 70 Joh7:11 | 101 Mr6:9 | 132 Mt24:30 |
| 71 Joh7:24 | 102 Mt21:3 | 133 Lu22:15 |
| 72 Joh7:31 | 103 Zec9:9 | 134 Lu22:17 |
| 73 Joh9:16 | 104 Lu19:38 | 135 Joh13:18 |
| 74 Joh9:17 | 105 Lu19:40 | 136 Joh13:21 |
| 75 Joh9:25 | 106 Lu19:42 | 137 Mt26:25 |
| 76 Joh9:27 | 107 Lu19:43,44 | 138 Joh13:27 |
| 77 Joh9:28,29 | 108 Joh12:19 | 139 Lu22:19 |
| 78 Joh9:30-34 | 109 Mt21:15 | 140 Lu22:20 |
| 79 Joh9:35 | 110 Ps8:2 | 141 Lu22:29,30 |
| 80 Joh9:36 | 111 Mr11:14 | 142 Isa45:18 |
| 81 Joh9:36 | 112 Mr11:17 | 143 Joh13:34 |
| 82 Joh9:37 | 113 Joh12:23,24 | 144 Joh14:27 |
| 83 Joh9:38 | 114 Joh12:27 | 145 Joh14:28 |
| 84 Joh9:39 | 115 Joh12:28 | 146 Joh14:30 |
| 85 Joh9:40 | 116 Joh12:28 | 147 Joh14:31 |
| 86 Joh9:41 | 117 Joh12:30,31 | 148 Joh17:3 |
| 87 Lu10:17 | 118 Joh12:34 | 149 Mt26:38 |
| 88 Lu10:23,24 | 119 Mt21:41 | 150 Mt:26:38 |
| 89 Lu10:21 | 120 Mt22:14 | 151 Mt26:39 |
| 90 Joh11:7 | 121 Mt22:28 | 152 Mt26:39 |
| 91 Joh11:8 | 122 Mr12:24,25 | 153 Mt26:40,41 |
| 92 Joh11:14 | 123 Mt22:36 | 154 Mt26:41 |
| 93 Joh11:16 | 124 Mt22:37-39 | 155 Mt26:45 |
| 94 Joh11:21-27 | 125 Mt23:38 | 156 Mt26:45,46 |
| 95 Joh11:32 | 126 Mt24:2 | 157 Mt26:49 |
| 96 Joh11:34 | 127 Mt24:3 | 158 Mt2650 |
| 97 Joh11:36 | 128 Mt24:7 | 159 Lu22:48 |
| 98 Joh11:37 | 129 Mt24:32-34 | 160 Joh18:4 |
| 99 Joh12:5 | 130 Mt24:14 | 161 Joh18:5 |
| 100 Mr14:6-8 | 131 Mt35:31,32 | 162 Joh18:8 |

[163] Joh18:8

[164] Lu22:49

[165] Mt26:54

[166] Joh18:11

[167] Mt26:55,56

[168] Joh18:20,21

[169] Joh18:22,23

[170] Mr14:58

[171] Mr14:60

[172] Mt26:63

[173] Mr14:62

[174] Mt26:65,66

[175] Mt26:68

[176] Lu22:70

[177] Lu22:70

[178] Joh18:31

[179] Joh18:31

[180] Joh18:33

[181] Joh18:34

[182] Joh18:35

[183] Joh18:35

[184] Joh18:36

[185] Joh18:36

[186] Joh18:37

[187] Joh18:37

[188] Joh18:38

[189] Lu22:4

[190] Lu22:5

[191] Lu23:14-16

[192] Mt27:25

[193] Mt27:46

[194] Mr15:35

[195] Lu23:46

[196] Joh19:30

[197] Mt28:10

[198] Joh20:17

[199] Rev12:7-9

[200] Rev6:2

# MY LIFE BY JESUS CHRIST
## A STORY

"My Life" has regenerated interest and
discussion about the true nature of Christ
and his life means to us, today.

We invite you to join in this discussion.

### TO ORDER THE BOOK
### SIMPLY CALL   1 800 247 6553

Special discounts and free shipping for your book club
or group, are available at our website.

For more information, author comments, or to join the
discussion,

Visit our website  **www.quietpublishing.com**

Watch for further pulications from Quiet Publishing
that strike to the heart of life.

We appreciate your involvement.

QUIET PUBLISHING

LOS ANGELES Q TORONTO